When Love Hurts

Aderonke Moyinlorun

AdomPublishers
Illinois. Indiana

Copyright © 2013 by Aderonke Moyinlorun
ISBN-13: 978-0615893907
ISBN-10: 0615893902
First Printing, 2013

AdomPublishers
Indianapolis,
IN46224
Tel: 812-233-3638

This edition is printed and bound in the United States of America by Createspace, Charleston SC.

For Tommy
This book is all yours...with love.

ACKNOWLEDGEMENTS

I would like to thank some special people:

My parents, Joseph & Victoria, thank you for being amazing.

Uncle Isaac, thank you being such a fan of my work. Your support is encouraging.

My extended family at AdomPublishers, thank you for your enthusiasm and hard work.

My readers, thank you for supporting my work. For whatever reason you all love me, I appreciate it. It's because of you that I can't stop writing. You have no idea how your very existence has added so much meaning to my life. Thank you so much.

Chapter 1

Tamara Price didn't want to get up from bed. As usual, she hadn't slept well. Actually, she hadn't been sleeping well for months now. She could cover up the dark circles beneath her eyes with makeup and hide the weight loss by purchasing smaller-sized clothes, but nothing could be done to offer her sanctuary from the forlorn feeling of being alone, a feeling she had known ever since Raymond Brock walked out of her life without any explanation or goodbye. And even though she had tried everything to avoid being alone, she still felt alone whenever she lay on this damn bed. She had worked hard, twenty-four hours a day seven days a week, until her colleagues forced her into taking this stupid vacation. She didn't want this vacation, but her colleagues refused to listen. Perhaps, they could tell she was miserable.

Her bedside phone rang, disrupting her thoughts. Rolling onto her back, she stretched a hand to pick up the phone. "Yes this is Ms. Tamara Price...No, I'm on vacation until next week...I understand. Tell Drake to go ahead and handle the case. I'm certain he'll handle it well...Thank you...That's fine...Bye for now."

She dropped the phone, seriously contemplating pulling the covers over her head and staying that way for the next three days. She'd done it before. That fateful morning when she woke up to the harsh reality of the other side of love. She had woken up from a peaceful sleep, on a Saturday morning, to a beautiful dawn. After breakfast, she'd sat down to watch TV when she heard the shocking news. She could still remember every word: *Raymond Brock, host of the syndicated talk show, Hello America, is officially off the market after marrying Dahlia Taylor in a small wedding in Paris.* For three days, she had stayed in bed without talking to anyone. Each day, the pain in her heart deepened.

Swallowing, she fought tears that seemed to come so easily every time she thought of Raymond. And even though it had been a year since the incident, it still hurt as if it was yesterday. Pain knotted Tamara's heart. She drew up her knees as if that would make the pain go away. She had managed to lock up the pain all this while, and was still capable of keeping it locked, she told herself.

Almost when she finally decided to pull the covers over her head and stay in bed, she heard her door opened. Startled, she rose and sat up to see who it was.

"Drake, you scared me!" she screeched.

"Oh sorry," Drake said, his voice not quite apologetic.

"You do not enter my bedroom! I thought it was someone else!"

He laughed, walking over to sit beside her on the bed. "You live in a gated, security-conscious neighborhood, and you're scared of an intruder?"

She scoffed and tossed her hair over her shoulder. "Risks of the job, I guess."

"Well yeah, risks of being the best divorce attorney in town! And with your track record of 'fixing' people's marriages, the only thing they'll ever be tempted to break into your house for would be to surprise you with a fruit basket and a bouquet of flowers. Unless, of course, your client is a mafia boss, then you're looking at a horse's head!"

"Okay, smartass! Why're you here? You could have called."

Drake grabbed her arm and pulled her out of bed. "I know you're going to sleep away your three-day break. So I got you something to do instead." He pushed her toward the bathroom. "Go get ready. Our last client, Tiffany and John, are renewing their vows today. You're going to be there."

She struggled. "Drake, you know I don't like to attend such events."

"Too late. I told them you'll be there." He pushed her into the bathroom and shut the door.

Tamara and Drake became very close back in high school, and then in college at University of Maryland in Baltimore. They went to law school together. After graduation, Tamara had decided to start her law firm, and Drake offered to join her. They had been together since then and been through a lot together. Drake was about six-four, two hundred pounds, with caramel skin. He was good looking and was good with women too.

"Alright, Tamara," Drake said, raising his voice enough for her to hear him. "I've got to rush back to work. See you later."

"Hey, who was that lady who called my home phone from the office? She said something about a client," Tamara said, raising her voice, too.

"That must be Sherry. She's an intern."

"Are you kidding me? You hired a female intern?"

"Yeah. What's the prob?"

"You can't screw a colleague or a client. You know that, right?"

"I'm not planning to have sex with her. And FYI, Tamara, I don't have sex with every woman I set my eyes on."

"All those girls you screwed in college? I'll say yes, you sleep with every woman you set your eyes on."

He laughed. "I haven't slept with you yet."

"I'm your boss, Drake!"

"It doesn't matter."

"Shut up, Drake," she yelled. "And get out of my room."

"Yes, boss." He bowed sarcastically and exited her room.

****

Tamara pulled into the parking lot. A crowd of about a hundred people stood outside the church. The church bell tolled as the people made their way inside the building. Tamara got out of the car and took a good look at herself before joining the horde of guests. She was wearing a white, figure-hugging Calvin Klein dress and heels as high as the Chrysler building. At thirty-two, Tamara had the body of a model. She was about five-feet, four-inches tall. She was slim, but had curves in all the right places. She was dark-skinned, bold and very beautiful.

An old woman spotted Tamara, nudged an old man next to her and whispered, "It's her. It's the woman!" At the sound of this, the rest of the crowd turned around, and when they saw Tamara, they started whispering to one another. As she got closer, the whispers got louder until they became murmurs. Realizing what was happening, Tamara tried to step away from the crowd.

The old lady who first spotted Tamara came to her, extending her hand. She touched Tamara's hand, looked deep into her eyes and with the softest voice, she said, "Thank you so much for saving their marriage. My daughter does not stop talking about how wonderful you were during that tough period. We owe you a huge debt of gratitude." Tamara didn't know how to respond. She could only smile. The old lady wiped a tear from her eyes as she made her way into the auditorium. A man came from within the church and told them the bride would be arriving soon, so they needed everyone inside the church for her grand arrival. The crowd hastily made its way into the auditorium, taking their seats.

The wedding procession entered the auditorium to a rapturous reception of applause and whoops. The couples exchanged their vows, and when the ceremony neared its end, the groom was given the microphone to give the vote of thanks. After speaking for a short while, he looked in Tamara's direction.

"...besides God there is one more person we'd love to thank; and that's Miss Tamara Price. At a time when Tiffany and I were going through a tough period in our marriage, we turned to you to help make our divorce as amicable as humanly possible. Instead, you managed to solve our problems and heal us, something that not even our marriage counselors or parents could achieve. You were more than a counselor; you were a friend and present help in our time of need. We wouldn't be here right now if it wasn't for you. So once again, from the bottom of our hearts, thank you."

The whole congregation erupted into a standing ovation, with those near Tamara shaking her hand while others kissed and hugged her. For a moment, she felt happy. After a long time of unhappiness, she told herself that she deserved it. People appreciated her, and that was enough. It reminded her of why she loved her job. When she lost Raymond, it felt as if her whole world had crashed. She tried everything to be happy again, but nothing worked. Until she decided that maybe she wasn't supposed to be happy. Maybe it was enough to make others happy. Still, it was ironic how she wasn't capable of keeping a man, but was capable of fixing people's marriages.

She wiped a tear from her eyes and then muttered, "Thank you" toward the groom as he blew a kiss in her direction.

Her mobile began to vibrate. She took it out, but ignored the caller. Shortly afterwards, it started vibrating again. She took it out and discreetly answered it.

"What is it?"

"Tamara, it's Drake."

"I know. What?"

"We've got a new client. Get over here right now!"

His voice was so tense Tamara could notice it through the phone.

"Drake, I'm on vacation. Handle it," she ordered, trying to keep her voice low.

"Dammit, Tamara! I wouldn't call you if it wasn't absolutely necessary."

"Who is the client?" she inquired.

He was quiet for a while. Tamara heard him take a deep breath. After a short silence, he managed to respond, "Raymond. The client is Raymond Brock!"

Chapter 2

Tires squealing in sensitive anger, Tamara pulled up at the parking lot. Very quickly, she got out of the car and walked toward the building. Her heart was pounding, and she didn't know how she would be able to stand before Raymond, the man who showed her love and then left her to wander the earth alone. She didn't want to imagine how her meeting with Raymond was going to be. He was just another client and she would treat him only as such, she thought to herself.

When she got to the lobby, all her employees were standing there waiting for her. She had only three employees; Megan, Sherry and Drake. Megan was a lawyer who became part of Tamara Price & Associates after Tamara had helped fixed her marriage. She was in her early thirties, but looked 21. More than anything else, Megan paid attention to her looks. Her blond hair was always perfect, never rough or unkempt.

Sherry was the intern just hired by Drake. She had just finished law school, and it was like a dream come true for her to get a job at Tamara

Price & Associates. She had always admired Tamara from afar. Tamara was her idol. And not only hers. Tamara was a big deal in law school. Most students admired her. Whenever her name was mentioned, it gave students goose bumps. Sherry particularly admired her strength and courage, and had always wondered what her driving force was.

When Tamara reached the lobby, she took a key out of her purse and tossed it to Sherry. "Go to my house. Get me a change of clothes."

She caught the key. "Okay."

As Sherry hurried away, Tamara took a good look at her. With a chiding expression, she raised her voice at Sherry. "Your skirt is too short, exposing too much skin."

"Ahem...I'm sorry..." she tried to explain, but Tamara had stopped listening. Her attention had shifted to Megan. "Megan," she called. "Make a list of our new clients. Let me have it within the hour."

"I'm on it!"

Tamara then glanced at Drake. "Drake," she called, and then was quiet for a second. "Just do something. Make yourself useful."

He smiled. "Yes, boss."

Tamara walked speedily into her office, where Raymond was waiting. She pushed the door open, and when her eyes fell on him, she felt her breath catch for an instant. She managed to pull herself together, reminding herself that he was just another client. Nothing more, nothing less.

Strangling the urge to walk over to him and

slap him hard across his face, asking him why he betrayed her, she walked calmly toward him and extended a hand in greeting. "Mr. Raymond Brock, welcome to Tamara Price & Associates."

"I've been waiting for an hour. I didn't think you were the type that would come in late to work," Raymond said, ignoring her greeting.

The hardened familiar voice crawled like ice down Tamara's spine, reviving the anger she had been trying so hard to suppress. Pride and irritation took over her sense of self and she walked past him, giving him an obvious head roll to let him know she clearly had an attitude.

"I own this place, meaning I can come to work anytime. And last time I checked, I do not report to you," she snapped.

"Are you always this rude to your clients?"

Tamara couldn't keep a throttling grip on her temper anymore. His words had kindled a flare of anger that she knew he read on her face.

Taking few steps closer to him, she glared at him. "How dare you, Raymond?" she asked. The palm of her hand became a fist as she tried not to hit him. "How dare you? You want to talk about being rude. You! You have the guts to talk to my face that I'm rude to you. I gave you everything, did everything and I thought we were okay. I thought we were alright. I thought our relationship was great. And then you run off to Paris to marry my best friend. You didn't break up with me. You didn't tell me what I did wrong. You just left. And now you have the nerve to tell me that I'm rude to you?"

She had let it all out, but didn't feel better. Instead, she wanted to say more. She wanted to let him know how much he'd hurt her. Her heart heaved in her chest and tears started to collect at the corners of her eyes.

"Raymond, you..."

"Mara!" he called very gently, cutting her off.

The way he called her brought back a familiar feeling. Mara. He alone called her that. Hearing it again reminded her of the good old times. And even though they were supposed to be good memories, it brought her even more pain. "Stop calling me that," she said with tears in her voice.

He touched her hand so gently that her whole body responded to his familiar touch.

Very quickly, she jerked his hand off. "Don't. Touch me." She looked at him with the intent of glaring at him. His brown eyes came boldly to hers. And for the first time since she entered the office, their eyes met. The connection was so intense that it threatened to drain every resistance in her. And damn! Did the man have to still be this handsome? He stood six-feet, three-inches tall and straight, with caramel skin. His bright brown eyes were daring and addictive. His dark hair was neatly cut and the suit he had on fitted him well. She could smell his cologne. Eternity by Calvin Klein. She recognized the smell. She had chosen the cologne for him when they first started dating. That he was still wearing the cologne she had chosen for him made her thought that maybe he still had a thing for her.

Their faces were already so close that she could feel his warm breath on her skin. For a moment, she thought he might kiss her. She needed to move away, but she couldn't. The intense connection she felt with this man had drained any resistance she had. His lips almost touched hers when they heard a light knock on the door. They quickly separated and took few steps away from each other as they glanced at the door. It was Anita, Raymond's personal assistant.

"I'm sorry. Did I intrude on something?"

"Oh! No. You're fine," Tamara responded very quickly. Tamara and Anita got along okay when Tamara was with Raymond, and they exchanged warm greetings. After they had talked for few seconds, Anita turned to Raymond. "Your show will be airing live in less than two hours. We should get going."

"Alright. We'll leave in a few."

"Okay," she said as she left the room, shutting the door behind her.

Once Anita left, Raymond turned to Tamara. "We should set a time and a place. We need to sit down and have a long talk."

"You know what? Forget that I mentioned anything about the past. We don't need to talk about anything."

A small sigh escaped his lips. "Ah! Mara, please, let me explain."

"How can I help you? Why are you here?" she asked, ignoring his pleas.

"MARA," he growled with a deep ultra-sexy voice. "Please, stop this attitude," he said very gently, emphasizing the 'please.'

"How can I help you?" she asked again, her voice hardened. She was back to treating him like any other client.

He was quiet for one long second, and then shrugged. "Okay, if that's what you want."

Tamara folded her arms across her chest, listening intently to whatever he had to say.

"I want a divorce from Dahlia," he started. "And I want you to handle it. Make the divorce as amicable as humanly possible."

She released her folded arms and drew slightly back. "Are you kidding me? I'm your ex."

He nodded. "I know."

"And you think I'd like to have anything to do with your marriage?"

"Yes, I think so."

She gave a sarcastic smile. "You're joking."

"No."

"Well, I can't help you. I have a reputation. I don't get people divorced; I fix marriages."

"That's a lie, and you know it. You're a divorce attorney. You've helped two or three couples get a divorce, and you've done it well."

"I only do that when the marriage is beyond saving."

"Well, mine is beyond saving."

"You don't determine that, I do. And I'm saying I can't help you. I don't want to help you."

He shrugged. "Okay, but promise me one thing."

"What?"

"Should Dahlia come to you, asking you to

save her marriage, you won't accept the case."

She chuckled. "Oh! So you want a divorce, but your wife doesn't want one. And you're afraid she might come running to me for help, and you decided to get to me first." He didn't reply, so she continued, "Don't worry. I don't have to promise you anything. Dahlia won't come to me. I'm certain."

"Mara,"

She cut him off. "Okay. Mr. Brock, this meeting is over." Walking past him, she held the door open for him. He walked to the door, but when he got to where she stood, he halted. Before he could say anything, Tamara gave another of her sarcastic smiles. "Good day, Mr. Brock. Hope to never see you again."

He took a long, gentle look at her, and then walked out of the office.

****

Not even midday yet, Tamara thought to herself, *and my day has already been flushed down the toilet.* Meeting Raymond had ruined her day. Worse, he had tried to kiss her, and she hadn't tried to stop him.

Sherry brought her some clothes, and she changed from her dress to something more formal—a white, Calvin Klein cowl-neck top over a cashmere-colored dress pants. As she sat in her office, her conscious mind bowed to her will, focusing on how to help out her clients. No matter how hard she tried, her subconscious made clear her total lack of control, as thoughts of Raymond continued to creep into her mind. She thought she had outgrown this feeling for Raymond. All this while, all she felt when she thought of Raymond was pain. And now that she saw him again, she felt different. The pain was still there, but there was yet another feeling she wasn't willing to admit.

The door opened, disrupting her thoughts. She glanced at the door to see who it was.

"Drake," she called.

"Tamara, Momma is here."

She rolled her eyes at him. "Your momma is dead. You didn't tell me she came back from the grave."

"Actually, I meant your momma is here."

"What!"

Tamara rushed out of her office. Could her day get any worse? When Momma showed up impromptu like this, something was definitely wrong.

Tamara and her mom shared a striking resemblance. She looked like her mom, except with laugh lines. And she had inherited everything from her mother, too, from her intelligence to her temper.

"Hi, Momma," she said as she walked into the lobby and into the welcoming embrace, returning it with a fierceness that had her mother narrowing her eyes in concern.

"Hi, yourself," she replied. "You alright?"

"I'm alright. It's just work."

"Well, it's a hot day, and I'm thirsty. Get me

something to drink."

"Okay."

In a split second, Sherry got her a bottle of water. When they walked into Tamara's office, Sherry placed the bottle and a cup on the table. Before she could walk out of the office, Tamara introduced Sherry to her mom. They exchanged greetings, and she left.

"So what you say happened at work?" her mother asked.

"C'mon, Momma, you know I can't tell. It's confidential."

"Everything is always confidential."

"How is business lately?" Tamara asked, trying desperately to change the subject.

"It's okay," she replied. "I still need to hire a fashion consultant. Most customers need help knowing what shoes match their dress."

Her mother went for the bottle of water while Tamara tried to go through the stack of documents on her table. A few seconds later, her mother threw the question that finally ruined her day.

"Have you seen Dahlia lately?" her mother asked.

She dropped the documents in her hands. "Dahlia Brock? The woman who ran off to Paris to get married to my boyfriend? No, I haven't seen her. And I don't want to ever see her."

"She is married to your ex-boyfriend," she corrected.

Before Tamara could respond, her phone signaled that she had a text. She reached for her phone. *Hey girl, let's hang out. Will be at your place in a few. Dahlia.*

She glanced at her mother, strangling the urge to yell at her. "You talked to Dahlia. You talked to the woman who destroyed my relationship."

"It's been a year, Tamara. Dahlia apologized to you at the time. She came by my store again today to apologize. I know it's difficult, but you've got to forgive her."

Her palm reflexively became a fist and hit the table. "Don't talk to me about forgiveness, Momma!" She jumped to her feet, scowling. "You're the one training to become a pastor in your church. You're the one who has to forgive everyone who hurts you. Not me! So don't ever ask me to forgive Dahlia! I do not forgive!" she yelled.

"Don't get grown with me, child. You better lower your tone. I can still get up from this damn chair and kick your butt. Now sit your butt back down and let's talk like reasonable adults."

Tamara sat back gently.

"I'm not asking that you and Dahlia be best friends again. I'm saying forgive her. Don't hold no grudges against her. Say hello to her if you run into her anywhere. She needs you to help save her marriage. Help save her marriage. Do your job."

"My job is to get people divorced, not to save marriages."

"But you've helped out quite a number of couples,"

"Yes, but that's not my job. My job is to get couples divorced. I'm capable of solving problems in marriages because I know the ups and downs of relationships. I've had my share of heartbreaks. And at thirty-two, I'm still single, alone and unmarried. When you were my age, you already had three marriages. As my momma, you should be worried that I'm still single. Instead, you're here giving me a lecture on forgiveness." She paused, but before her mother could reply she said, "Momma, how could they allow you to train to become a pastor after three failed marriages?"

"Don't insult me!"

For the next few seconds, silence covered the room

"Tamara," her mother called. Her voice had softened up a bit. "You know I'm worried that you're still single. And I always pray that God gives you the right man at the right time. But you have to forgive first. Forgive Dahlia. Help her save her marriage. And that's it. It's simple."

"Okay," Tamara said quietly. She only agreed with her mother just to make her stop talking about it, but over her dead body would she forgive Dahlia or help save her stupid *stupid* marriage, a marriage that shouldn't have happened in the first place.

"I suggest you rush home very quickly. Don't keep her waiting for too long."

Tamara's eyes flicked up to look at her mother. "What?"

"Yeah, you heard me. Go and listen to what

Dahlia has to say."

Tamara pulled her eyebrows together in a frown. "I'll see her after work."

Chapter 3

All Raymond Brock wanted to do was rip off his tie, grab a beer and get drunk. He had just finished hosting the show, *Hello America*, and his performance was below average. But that didn't bother him at all. All that bothered him was that he had hurt her. He had hurt Tamara Price too much, perhaps more than he could ever understand. That was the only reasonable explanation for her sudden coldness. Tamara used to be a soft and gentle person. To see her suddenly become cold and emotionless was still something he couldn't understand.

As he stepped inside his office, Raymond vowed that as soon as that day's work was over, he would go back to Tamara's office. He needed to talk to her. He didn't mind if she walked him out of her office again. All that mattered was that he was going to try and ease her pain. She had carried it alone for too long.

Shrugging out of his suit jacket, he sat on his armchair and pulled his tie loose. He poured himself a glass of water as his thoughts went back to Tamara. Well, he had never been able to get her out of his mind.

He remembered the start, when he'd met her. From the first glance, he was hypnotized by the attraction that had kept intensifying. From their first conversation, he'd sunk into a well of affection, perhaps the deepest he'd ever known. It was magical how they'd connected and craved for each other. She had aroused his every emotion, appeased his every need. And he had ruined everything. He had betrayed their love when he married Dahlia. If only Tamara would hear him out, he'd explain and make her understand his reason.

But Tamara hated him now. A bitter taste rose from his gut to his mouth at this thought. When he saw her today, every look of resentment she gave him made his heart want to explode, first with the need to soothe her, then with fury at himself for ruining what they had.

A light knock on the door brought him back to the present.

His personal assistant thrust her head into the room. "May I come in?"

"Come in, Anita."

Raymond took a quick look at Anita as she walked into the office. From the look on her face, he could tell something was bothering her. "What's the problem?" he asked, with concern written all over his face.

Anita wanted to sit, but then decided against it. "Sir, your performance today on the *Hello America* show was not impressive. In fact, if I want to be honest, it was bad."

Raymond hissed and relaxed back on his armchair. "Is that why you got all worked up? C'mon, Anita, it's nothing. I'm sure the audience can forgive one not quite impressive performance."

"Actually, it's two unimpressive performances. Your first show after your wedding was awful. And today was awful, too. So you have two terrible performances to your name. And you're a top TV personality. You can't afford to keep messing up every time. If care is not taken, people will stop watching you and the ratings will drop and…"

He cut her off. "Don't worry, Anita. It won't get to that."

Tapping her artificial nail on the table, she was quiet for a while. After a few seconds of silence, she narrowed her gaze at Raymond. "Is this about Tamara Price?"

Raymond didn't give a response.

"Sir, if I may speak as a friend for a minute…"

Raymond considered for a moment. "Go ahead."

She nodded and sat gently on the armchair opposite him. "I've been your PA and confidant for almost three years, and I can say that I know one or two things about you." She swallowed before continuing. "I know you loved Tamara Price, but you know why you dumped her for Dahlia. You've been married to Dahlia for a good one year, and you've been doing fine without Tamara Price. I believe if Ms. Price was a very good woman, you wouldn't have left her for

Dahlia…"

Raymond's caution flared. "Don't you dare talk about Tamara like that!" Realizing that he had unnecessarily yelled at her, he went calm. After a while, he let out a breath and began again. "I loved Tamara Price. I still do. She is the love of my life, my heartbeat. Even you, Anita, you ought to understand that."

"She's not your heartbeat. With all due respect, you haven't seen her in the last year and your heart has been working fine."

"My heart hasn't been working fine. Actually, I've been suffering in silence."

Anita lowered her head in thought and let out a deep breath. When she brought her head back up, her eyes darted briefly to Raymond. "I get it. You love Tamara Price. I'm a woman. I understand what love is. But the fact that you love Tamara doesn't mean you have to destroy your career. Sit back and think again. You'll see that there is at least a little sense in what I'm saying. I'm asking you to take everything slow; don't push it too hard. If Tamara is meant to be yours, she'll be yours, and you don't have to lose your career to get her back."

"Okay," Raymond said.

Anita glanced skeptically at him. "Okay?"

He nodded. "Yes, okay. I'll take your advice."

A smile spread across her face. "That was easier than I thought. I'm glad you're taking my advice." She stood from the armchair. "Is there anything you might need me to do for you?"

"Yes, of course." He concentrated his gaze on

the stack of documents on his table, trying to avoid looking at her. "Find out what time Tamara Price leaves her place of work."

"What! I thought you were taking my advice to let it go."

He didn't respond. A knowing grin spread across his face.

Anita glanced at him, hit her forehead with her palm and walked away in disappointment.

****

Raymond Brock had waited in his car outside of Tamara's office building for only two hours, but his uneasiness grew with each passing hour. Would she listen to him? Would she ignore him?

He took a deep breath and almost fell asleep when he noticed Tamara walk out of the building. Even in the near darkness, his eyes could still catch the frame of Tamara. As fast as he could, he hurried out of his car and ran toward her. When he was only a few strides away, he slowed down and walked very gently to her.

"Hi," he said quietly, still breathing a little hard from his run.

She didn't turn to look at him. "Hi," she replied gently.

The calm in her voice surprised him, but he covered his surprise as best as he could. He stood there for a while, hands in his pocket. His eyes didn't leave Tamara for a second. She was still as beautiful as he remembered.

Tamara had a stack of documents in her right

hand and a large purse on the other, making it difficult for her to lock the door. Raymond contemplated helping her as she struggled with the door, but scared that she might turn down his help in a very rude manner, he hesitated. But then he summoned up the courage. "Let me help you," he offered.

"No, but thanks."

The way she was being polite with him was eating him up inside. He longed for the intimacy that they shared; the affection that once sprouted between them. He'd give anything for them to go back to the way it used to be.

He continued to watch her struggle with locking the door, and when he couldn't stand seeing her struggle alone anymore, he offered to help again. "You need help. Let me help you."

"I can handle it!" she yelled. "I've been handling it before now. Alone."

Finally, she locked the door and turned to leave. As she walked away, Raymond followed. After taking two or three steps, she stopped abruptly and glared at him.

"What is it you want?"

Even though she was glaring at him, he could still see the kindness behind the glare.

"I..." he began and then stopped dumbly, afraid of saying the wrong thing.

Her glare deepened, waiting.

Raymond started over, keeping his voice low. "You know, I had a whole speech rehearsed in my mind. But now, seeing you, I can't remember a word of it. You have that much effect on me."

The sound of his voice vibrated with something deep inside her, weakening her a little. She swallowed hard and tried to put up the pretense that she didn't care one bit. "Raymond, you still haven't told me what you want."

"Please, let me take you to the nearest restaurant. Let's talk over dinner."

"I remember telling you this afternoon that our meeting is over. Don't you get it?"

"This is not a meeting, Mara. It's..." He hesitated a while. "It's like a date."

"I'm not dating," she said and began walking to her car.

Raymond followed. "Mara!"

"I mean it, Raymond. I'm not dating. For now." She stopped walking and turned to look at him. "And even if I want to date, not with you," she said, her voice now very soft, almost kind.

"I don't understand. Why can't you eat dinner with me?"

She lifted her shoulders in a shrug. "Because we were lovers once."

She said it as if they could never be lovers ever again.

"Once?" he asked.

"Yes, once. Get it, Raymond. I'm your ex. You and I can never be. Ever again. Go back to your wife."

Raymond took her hand, ever so gently, and raised it to his lips. Pressing a kiss against the skin of her hand, he held her hands far longer than was proper.

His touch sent vibrations through her,

impaling her with its power. She gave him a sidelong glance, eyeing him with suspicion. "And just what are you doing?"

He gave her a wicked smile. "Wooing you back to my arms."

She looked at him for a while, and then walked away.

****

Tamara parked in her garage. When she stepped out of the car, her eyes caught a glimpse of Dahlia standing at her front door. It must have felt like a death sentence to Dahlia as she walked over, because when Tamara got into her eyesight, Dahlia looked scared, as if she was afraid of her.

"Hey, Tamara," Dahlia said.

Tamara said nothing. She just walked past Dahlia and inserted the key into the lock.

"Look, Tamara, can I talk to you?"

She held opened the door for her. "Make it quick."

Dahlia walked in cautiously, but Tamara didn't offer her a seat. Tamara stood opposite of her, folded her arms around her chest and listening intently to whatever Dahlia had to say.

"How are you these days?"

"Fine." Tamara answered quickly and bluntly.

"I want to get straight to the point..."

Tamara cut her off. "Please, do."

"It's been one year since our fight. We haven't talked or called or anything, and I want to put an end to it."

"I didn't start the fight. You did. You're the one who ran off to Paris to marry my boyfriend."

"And I'm very, very sorry for that. What happened between Raymond and I was…"

Tamara cut her off again. "Save it. I don't want to know what happened."

Dahlia was quiet for a while. She was confused on what to say next.

Meanwhile, her presence was suffocating Tamara. She wanted Dahlia out of her house very quickly. Not only out of her house, but out of her life. Forever. The sight of Dahlia reminded her of what a failure she was as a woman. She had wondered what Raymond found attractive about Dahlia. She had known Dahlia since childhood, and she knew everything about her. Dahlia was bold and beautiful. She was light-skinned, with curves in the right places. Tamara had always known Dahlia to be a woman who could not survive on her own, except with the help of a man. If your rich boyfriend was still faithful, that's only because he hadn't met Dahlia yet. Dahlia knew her way around men. She could seduce them into her lap and into doing anything she wanted. Was that how she seduced her Raymond? The question popped up in Tamara's head, and it sickened her for a moment that even Raymond couldn't resist her charms.

With an obvious look of resentment, Tamara asked, "So what do you want from me now?"

"Forgiveness. I'm sorry, Tamara," she said.

But Tamara knew Dahlia well enough to know that she could never be truly sorry for anything.

"What exactly do you want from me, Dahlia?"

Dahlia tried to soften her voice and put on a repentant face. "Forgiveness. And your help in saving my marriage."

"Do I look like an idiot? Why would I want to do that for you? The only reason I'm talking to you right now is because my momma asked me to. And you have the guts to ask me to help you."

Tears filled Dahlia's eyes as she stared apologetically at Tamara. "I know I've offended you too much, and you're right if you don't want to help me." Her voice was shaky and unsure. "But please, help me. If not for my sake, for my son's sake. I don't want him to grow up without his daddy."

Tamara's heart felt as if it were coming up into her throat. She swallowed hard as she tried not to betray any emotion. "You have a son?"

"Yes. He's seven months old."

Tamara's mind did the math. Their marriage was only one year and they couldn't have had a seven-month-old baby. Unless. Of course, she was pregnant before the wedding. And that could only mean one thing. Raymond had been cheating on her with Dahlia long before their wedding.

Her heart felt as if it would explode. She just wanted to lie on her bed and cry. Alone. But she told herself that she wouldn't let Dahlia get to her. She couldn't show weakness in her presence.

Tamara considered for a while. She knew it was impossible to force two people to stay married if they didn't want to. Raymond had made it clear that he no longer wanted the marriage, but Dahlia did. She would try her best to help her for the baby's sake, and because her mother had pleaded with her, too. And how else could she make Raymond suffer, except to make him stay married to a woman he didn't love?

Tamara let out a breath. "Okay."

A smile spread across Dahlia's face. "Thank you."

"I'm not promising anything yet, but come to the office tomorrow morning. My team and I will take a look at your case."

"Thank you," she said with a soft smile. "Then, please, let's start afresh, a new relationship. I know it won't be like it used to for a while, but let's at least give it a try."

"Maybe, Dahlia. I'll think about it."

"Please, do."

Tamara gave a nod. Dahlia said her goodbye and Tamara closed the door after her.

Chapter 4

When Tamara Price strode into the conference room of Tamara Price & Associates, she noticed one thing: there was no conversation. None at all. Not that she had expected a party atmosphere in an office environment, but it was unusual for their gatherings to be quiet. Drake should be flirting with Megan, and Megan should be overreacting and screaming at Drake. That was how they managed to give their busy life a little fun.

Before Tamara could take a seat, Drake began, "We need to talk about the Brock case."

Tamara decided against sitting and threw her purse down on the chair. "There's nothing to discuss."

"There is something to discuss," Drake said. "Actually, there is a lot to discuss." He looked toward Sherry. "Sherry, you first. Tell us your opinion about this case."

Tamara folded her arms across her chest, listening.

"We're divorce attorneys," Sherry began, her

voice very shaky for fear of saying the wrong thing and looking stupid before the genius. "If Mr. Brock doesn't want this marriage anymore, I think we should get him the divorce. It's not right..." she stammered. "It's not right to force someone into a marriage he doesn't want. We can only fix this marriage if both of them are willing to make their marriage work. But since one person is not willing, then the only option is to get them divorced."

Megan shot Sherry a deadly look and then glanced at Tamara. "That woman, Dahlia Brock, she needs our help. And I don't know what's going on with you and why it's so difficult for you to take this case. I know this case is personal to you in some way. I know that this case is hurting you, and I'm very sorry. But we have to help that woman. She needs our help and..."

"You seem to forget that the husband doesn't want the marriage anymore," Sherry interrupted.

Megan frowned. "Don't talk to me about that!" she said, almost yelling. Megan's hard face softened as she glanced back at Tamara. "When I came running to you, asking you to help save my marriage, my husband was no longer interested in the marriage. But you did your thing, played your tricks and got us back together." She paused to swallow the lumps in her throat. "Before you helped me, you told me that what you're going to do might not save my marriage, but it's enough to try. So let's at least try to help Dahlia, even if it's not going to work out fine."

When Megan finished talking, everyone was

quiet. Tamara knew Megan was taking it too personally. Somehow, Megan saw herself in every woman whose home was about to break. Her emotional response to this case wasn't new to Tamara. Megan was always like that, always advocating for the woman.

Drake cleared his throat to have their attention. "I don't talk a lot, but my opinion is that we don't take this case. We don't help the husband. We don't help the wife."

Drake, Tamara thought to herself, is always trying to look out for her. Drake didn't want them to take the case because he knew everything that had happened between Tamara and Raymond. He knew how Raymond broke her heart. He knew how much pain Tamara suffered since the breakup.

Tamara unfolded her arms and glanced around. She let out a deep breath. "I made my decision last night. We are taking the case and Dahlia Brock is our client."

Drake responded with a long, silent stare. For a split second, no one said anything as the shock silenced them.

"Are you sure?" Drake asked.

"Absolutely," Tamara replied confidently.

A smile spread across Megan's face as she wiped the tears that had collected at the corner of her eyes.

Tamara took her phone and placed a call to Dahlia. Without any pleasantries, she cut to the chase. "You may come in," she said and quickly hung up.

In a split second, Dahlia walked into the conference room.

Megan welcomed her and led her to a seat.

Sitting at the edge of the table, Tamara started, "Dahlia, we've decided to take your case. Now, you're going to tell us what happened in your marriage. Don't hide anything."

Dahlia nodded and started. "Everything was fine. Raymond was loving...and caring, until all of a sudden, he started complaining that I don't contribute anything financially to the family. When we got married I told Raymond to let me work, but he refused. He said what he was earning would be enough. But suddenly, he started complaining. I tried to talk to him and remind him that he was the one who refused to let me work." She sighed, trying as much as possible not to make eye contact with anyone. "He stopped complaining about it for a while and I thought everything was fine again. So two days ago, I reminded him that 25th of next month is our one-year wedding anniversary and I suggested we have a party." Tears filled her eyes and she tried to hold it back. "But Raymond said a party wouldn't be necessary because he wanted a divorce." She glanced at Tamara. "Tamara, please, you have to help me."

Before Tamara had a chance to open her mouth, Drake jumped in. "You're saying you didn't cheat on your husband and your husband isn't having an affair and you two are screwing each other very well?"

"To the best of my knowledge, Raymond and I

were faithful to each other. And yes, our sex life was okay."

Drake smiled. "Then it's a simple case."

"Dahlia," Tamara called, staring closely into her eyes. "Are you sure that you've told us all of the truth and you're not hiding anything?"

She nodded.

"Good! Now, you will go back home and act as normal as possible. Don't bring up the divorce issue with your husband. If he asks you about it, tell him you need little time. If he starts an argument, don't argue with him. Be nice to him, be loving and caring. Take care of him. Show him love. Men can be hard, but they are soft on the inside. And don't be ashamed to let him see that you're hurt. Don't hide your red, puffy eyes from him. You don't have to pretend that you're okay with him asking for divorce. Pretense kills marriages."

Dahlia nodded in understanding.

Tamara shifted her gaze to Megan. "Megan, I need you to work with Dahlia and prepare a resumé. She needs a job a.s.a.p."

Megan shifted in her chair. "I'm on it."

"Drake, I need you to find out what Raymond Brock has been up to within the one year of his marriage. Where he's been, which hotel he's lodged at, who he spends each day with, how he spends his money. If you have to follow him every day, do it!"

"Copy that." He stood and began to head for the door. When he opened the door, he waited for both Megan and Dahlia to walk out.

"Drake!" Tamara called. He stopped and glanced at her. "You can't get sexually involve with a client. Don't forget the rules!"

He gave a sarcastic smile. "You told me to follow Raymond Brock. I'm sure he's a man. And the last time I checked, I wasn't gay."

She returned his smile. "Oh! Shut up." She winked at him. "Don't pretend as if you don't know who I meant."

"Yes, boss."

Tamara glanced around and saw Sherry still sitting there waiting for orders. "Sherry, you're still here."

"Yes," she said with a broad smile, expecting Tamara to tell her what to do.

"Just go and make yourself useful. A coffee for me."

Sherry gave her a look that said, *seriously? While others are on legal duties, I'm on coffee-making duty.*

****

Tamara sat in her office, working on the stack of documents sitting on her table. The cup of coffee delivered for her remained untouched. She had been working too hard. She couldn't stop. She didn't want to. The fear that she'd think about Raymond wouldn't let her. Giving all attention to her work would leave no space for Raymond. That was the only way she could keep the door of her heart shut so that Raymond wouldn't take up space inside.

Her eyes went to the door as she heard a light knock. Megan and Dahlia walked in.

"You have the resumé ready?" Tamara asked.

"I'm afraid not."

Tamara glared at Megan. "What?"

"It's not her," Dahlia said. "It's my fault. I don't have any job experience."

Tamara's glare withdrew itself. "Really?"

Megan nodded and handed her a folder. Tamara read through it very quickly and then glanced at Dahlia. "You don't have any job experience?" she asked again.

"I don't."

"And you don't have any special skills you can use to make money?"

She shook her head. "No. All I ever got paid for was for being pretty. I was a model when I was 14, but no modeling agency will hire me now. I'm in my early 30's. I'm too old for modeling."

Tamara wasn't surprised. She had known Dahlia since high school. She had the "I'm too cute to get myself dirty" attitude. She wouldn't take any job or work hard to earn her own bucks. She was absolutely dependent on others. At first, she was dependent on her parents for everything. And when they didn't seem capable of getting her all she wanted, she moved her dependency to her numerous boyfriends. And good for her, she had the power of seduction. She was capable of luring those men into her laps, wrapping them around those pretty little fingers of hers.

Tamara took a good look at Dahlia again. She was indeed a pretty woman, and was well-dressed, too. She wore a cream-colored top over a navy blue skirt. She had on cream-colored shoes, with a navy blue purse and other accessories. "Maybe you can still get paid for being pretty," Tamara said.

Dahlia gave a questioning look.

"Tell me, Dahlia, did you hire a fashion consultant?" Tamara asked.

"No, I chose my outfit myself,"

"Well, maybe you just got a job," she said as she grabbed her cellphone to make a call to her mother. "Hey, Momma, how you been today?"

"Child, working, that's all. What you over there doing?"

"Working, too. Momma, do you still want to hire a fashion consultant?"

"Yeah. You got someone for me?"

"Yeah. Dahlia."

"Dahlia? Are you sure you're okay with her working for me? You'll be running into her every now and then."

"It's absolutely okay with me."

"Okay, child. Send her over to me. I'll skip the interview. I trust your instinct. And I'm proud of you, honey."

"Thanks, Momma. Talk to you later." She hung up and smiled at Dahlia. "You just got a job."

"Thank you, Tamara," she replied, smiling. "When can I start?"

"As soon as possible."

"I'll let my husband know." Dahlia walked out of the room to make a quick call to her husband.

A few minutes later, she walked back into the room. From the look on her face, Tamara could already tell his response. "Did he say no?"

Dahlia gave a slow nod, face falling. "He said that he will pay me a huge amount for child and spousal support after the divorce, so there's no need to work."

Tamara's brow went up in disbelief. "Raymond said that?"

Dahlia nodded sadly.

Has the man gone mad? Tamara asked herself. *Does he think people only work because of money?* In this case, getting a job would get Dahlia some respect in her marriage and who was he to deny her that?

Angrily, she stood up, grabbed her purse and headed for the door.

"Where are you going?" Megan asked.

"To talk to someone."

Chapter 5

Pulling into the parking lot of MDNC TV station, Tamara glanced at herself and felt confident in the blue shirt she wore over a short black skirt. As she walked hurriedly in to the building, old feelings reemerged within her. She remembered her frequent visit to Raymond's office in the past. She remembered bringing lunch for Raymond every noon. And in the rare times she didn't bring lunch along, they'd go out to eat. It wasn't the lunch that mattered—it was the fact that they loved to spend every moment together. They couldn't do without each other.

Her anger disappeared into her feelings.

Even though she tried not to, she couldn't help remembering Raymond. She'd tried so hard to forget him. In the past few days, she'd reminded herself that Raymond meant nothing to her. He was just like any other client. But deep down in her heart, she knew she wasn't being entirely honest with herself.

She remembered when she first met him. Such a fool she'd been. She had been swept away by his charm. His loving and caring nature had melted her heart. She believed it when Raymond said he couldn't live without her. He'd often called her his heartbeat. A gentle smile ran across her face at the thought. But the smile quickly faded away when reality set in.

He'd run off to Paris to marry her best friend. He'd deceived her, used her and dumped her. Now that he'd returned, her pain and humiliation had doubled. Dahlia had the guts to ask her to save their marriage, and Raymond dared to ask her to be his divorce attorney. Tears gathered at the corner of her eyes, but she held it back, a chastising laugh gathering in her throat. He wasn't worth the tears.

"Hello, Tamara. How are you doing?"

Anita's voice broke through her reverie. Her lips curved into a smile as she gave Anita a friendly hug. "I'm doing alright. Yourself?"

"I'm doing okay, too." She took a quick look at Tamara. "You're looking good," she said. "Like always," she added with a smile.

At the compliment, Tamara smiled back, almost shyly. "You look good yourself.'

"Aww, thanks," she replied. "Here to see Mr. Brock?"

"Yes. I'm handling his divorce, though I'm trying to make sure they don't get divorced." Tamara suddenly felt the need to explain further so that Anita wouldn't think she was seeing Raymond for personal reasons.

Anita smiled. "You're good at what you do." The smile on her face disappeared very quickly as she glanced around to make sure no one was listening. "Tamara, I need to ask you a favor," she said, lowering her voice.

"Anything."

"You know, ever since Raymond came into your office to see you, he hasn't been himself. His performance on the show hasn't been his greatest."

Tamara nodded in agreement. "Yeah. I watched the show. I noticed it, too."

"Good." She hesitated a moment. "It's just that, you know, you both have history together. And..." She stammered to a halt and then swallowed. "I want you to please help talk to him. He'll listen to you. I'm just afraid that the ratings are going to drop soon, and he might lose sponsors for the show."

"I don't think I'm in the best position to talk to him about that."

"I know you are, Tamara. He listens to you."

Tamara lifted her shoulders in a shrug. "Okay. I'm not promising, but I'll try."

Smiling, Anita gave her a quick hug. "Thanks. Let me show you to his office."

Tamara followed as they walked down the hallway. When they got to his office, Anita opened the door and peeped in. "He's not here. I'm sure he's somewhere around. Wait inside, I'll go look for him."

"Alright, thanks."

Tamara waited in his office, her heart beating fast, scared of standing before the man she once loved. The man she still loved, but afraid to admit. But then she told herself to put her head before her heart. Pacing back and forth, she tried to align her heart with her head, telling herself over and over that Raymond meant nothing to her.

"Mara," Raymond called, "this is a surprise. I wasn't expecting you."

She stopped pacing and turned to look at him. When her eyes fell on him, her voice caught up in her throat.

He stood at the door for a while, studying her nervous face. His torrid gaze stared back at her. As if he already knew all there was to know just by gazing at her, he glanced back at Anita. "Leave us."

"Okay." Anita left and shut the door.

One step at a time, he walked gently toward her. He looked thinner than she'd last seen him. Perhaps he hadn't been eating well. Or maybe he hadn't been sleeping well. Her eyes went to his face, checking if he had any circles beneath his eyes that could indicate lack of sleep. Instead, her eyes caught the collar of his shirt. It was carelessly upturned. She felt the need to walk over to him and adjust his collar like she had always done in the past. The Lord help her! She missed him! She missed the man and the intimacy they once shared.

Raymond, now close to where she stood, suddenly made it hard for her to control her breathing. Taking one step away, she swallowed. "Your wife, Dahlia, feels you have no respect for her because she has no job; because she is not making any financial contribution to the family. I get it. You don't want the marriage anymore. And if there is going to be a divorce, you should at least give her the chance to get a job and then bow out of the marriage with her self-respect still intact. But you, Mr. Billionaire, think people only work to earn money, so you deny your wife the privilege to work, making false promises that you will pay a large amount of money for child and spousal support after a divorce. Marriage is much more than who pays the bills. I do not understand why you would stoop this low just to inflict pain on your wife."

Raymond's defenses rose up. He frowned. "Where is this coming from?" he demanded. "When Dahlia called to let me know she got a job, I didn't tell her not to take it. I said it's more reasonable if she doesn't start working yet. We have a seven months old baby, and I reasoned that it might be tough on her to combine work with taking care of our son. So, I told her that she can go ahead if she thinks she can handle it. And if not, I'll pay her more than enough money for child support after the divorce. She has nothing to worry about. When I said that, I was being considerate. I was on her side." Raymond controlled his temper and placed his hands in the pockets of his pants. "And I don't understand why you said I have no respect for my wife because she doesn't have a job. Honestly! That has never been an issue between myself and Dahlia. I don't have problems with taking care of my responsibilities, and I don't care if Dahlia has a dime to contribute or not. I can take care of my responsibility."

Tamara shot him a questioning look. "Are you saying that the reason you want a divorce is not because your wife doesn't have a job?"

Raymond pulled his brows together in a frown. "That would be outrageous. Unreasonable. Despicable."

"Enough of the grammar! If it's not because your wife doesn't have a job, then what is your reason for asking for a divorce?"

Taking out his hands from the pocket of his pants, he let out a breath. "I'm sorry, Mara. I can't tell you that. It's between myself and Dahlia. And I know that Dahlia understands my reason for wanting a divorce."

She didn't look at him, but nodded in agreement. "It's okay. Don't tell me. You want a divorce because your wife doesn't have a job. I know that. I shouldn't have asked you again. What was I expecting? That you would tell me the truth?" She shook her head slowly. "You're not capable of telling the truth. You've always been a liar. A very good liar."

A small sigh escape his lips. "Ah, Mara. Stop talking like this." He leaned closer to her, so that there was no longer space between them. "You've known me for a very long time. Do you actually think I'm capable of such a thing?"

Still not looking at him, a hint of emotions returned to her face. That Raymond was standing very close to her had triggered the current passing through her veins. She suddenly had trouble controlling her breathing. "It feels like I don't know you at all," she said gently, tears in her voice. "I never knew you. I don't know what you're capable of. The man I thought I knew wouldn't leave me for anybody."

He reached for her hand. At his touch, her heartbeat galloped in her chest. "Look at me, Mara," he said.

Tears gathered in her eyes, but she still wouldn't look at him. "Did you cheat on me with Dahlia? Were you with Dahlia at the same time you were with me?"

He held her face with both hands. "Look at me."

Finally, her eyes held him as firmly as his hands held her face. "Listen to me." His whisper was so low she had to concentrate to hear him. "I loved only you."

"Did you cheat on me with Dahlia?"

Continuing to watch her eyes, he put his face so close to hers that she could feel the warmth of his breath on her face. "I. Love. You."

Before she could respond, his lips touched hers. Her full lips parted and received him in a very deep kiss. In a split second, she broke it and slapped him hard across his face and backed away from him. "Player! I trusted you. I loved you," she yelled as tears filled her eyes.

Raymond walked over to her and kissed her again. This time, the kiss soothed her. It felt as if that was exactly what she needed at that moment. But it wasn't long when reason flooded back into her mind. She broke the kiss and without meeting Raymond's eyes, she pulled away and headed for the door.

"Mara," he called out, trying to stop her.

Placing her hand on the door knob, she stopped and let out a deep breath. "And the man I thought I knew always takes his job seriously, too."

****

"Drake!" Tamara's voice rocketed as she walked into the office.

Drake walked toward her, keeping a straight face. "Please, God, smite this evil witch."

Tamara ignored his sarcasm. "Get Megan and Sherry. The conference room. Now!"

In a few minutes, they were all present in the conference room. Tamara paced back and forth until they all settled down.

"Where are we on the Brock's case?" Tamara asked, folding hers arms across her chest as she stopped pacing.

Drake opened a folder and took out a document. "I managed to pull some strings and I got the Brock's phone records and emails. Everything seems okay. Nothing to indicate that either of them is having an affair."

Sherry suddenly gave a loud cough.

Tamara unfolded her arms and stared at her. "You okay, Sherry?"

She nodded. "Yes, I'm okay. But if I may say something..."

All attention shifted to her.

"Yes, go ahead," Tamara said.

"If we think one of them is having an affair, why don't we just ask them? That's better than digging on them and intruding on their private lives."

"From my experience, I've found out that if you want to know if a particular husband or wife is screwing around, the last person you ask is that particular husband or wife," Tamara replied.

"But they are our clients. If they say they're not having an affair, then they are not having an affair. It's our duty to trust them."

Tamara gave her a soft smile. "Trust has to be earned, my dear."

"That doesn't mean we can't trust them. It's not right..."

The glare that Tamara shot her felt like a scolding and she stopped talking.

"Look, Sherry," Tamara began, raising her voice. "One of the reasons why their marriage is crashing, one of the reasons they need our help is because they've been lying to each other. And I'm not talking about Dahlia and Raymond only. There are many marriages out there that are founded on deceptions and lies. Having an affair is not the only thing they lie about. They lie about everything. The wife lies that she likes her husband's boring jokes. The husband lies that he loves his wife's terrible cooking. And guess what? Lies are like ticking time bombs. At the appropriate time, they will explode. And when they do, people start running around trying to save their marriage. But they can't save it, because they continue to lie. They lie to family and friends, saying their marriage is okay. They lie to their marriage counselors, too. In the end, they end up ruining their marriage. One of the reasons I've been able to save a lot of marriages is because I'm not afraid to find out the truth by any means necessary. Do you understand that?"

Sherry shuddered and nodded very quickly.

Taking the documents from Drake, Tamara read through them very quickly. After a few minutes, she glanced at Drake. "Dahlia seems to be making a lot of calls to this number," she walked over to Drake and showed the document to him. "You know who owns the number?"

"One Steve Ryder."

Tamara raised a brow. "Who is Steve Ryder?"

"He works for the Brocks. He's on their domestic staff. Their gardener."

"Okay." Tamara put the documents into the folder and handed it back to Drake. "We didn't get anything from their phone records and emails. For the next few weeks, I want you to follow both of them. I want to know how they're spending their days. I want to know if they are screwing around." She pointed a finger at Drake. "Follow Raymond. Find out where he goes and how he spends his day."

"Yes, boss."

"Megan," she called. "Follow Dahlia."

"I'm on it," Megan said.

Tamara was quiet for a second and then she turned to Sherry. "Actually, I changed my mind. Sherry, you follow Dahlia."

Sherry's eyes went wide.

"Any problems?" Tamara asked.

She shook her head. "No. No problems."

"Good. Now get going."

Chapter 6

"Home, Hell Home," Raymond grunted under his breath as he pulled his Chrysler 300 into the driveway of his house and slammed on the brakes. No matter how much fun and stress he had at work, coming back home was something he never looked forward to. At all. Home was hell. Dahlia made sure of that.

When he got to the front door, he held his breath, contemplating whether to just go back out and hang out with his friends. But then he decided against it and opened the door.

"Hey, honey, you look so tired. How was your day?"

Raymond's eye popped in astonishment, looking around to see if there was someone else his wife could be talking to. "You talking to me?"

Dahlia smiled. "Yes. It's just you and I. Who else would I be talking to?"

"It's...just that..." he stammered to a halt.

Dahlia walked over to him and helped him take off his suit jacket. "Aww. You did great on Hello America today. I'm so proud of you."

Raymond was tongue-tied. What happened to his ice-queen wife? It seemed as if the ice queen had finally melted.

"I prepared dinner. It's your favorite," Dahlia said.

WOW! He'd give anything to come home into the welcoming embrace of this loving wife. He'd give anything to let things remain this way between them. Finally, it came to him that Dahlia had been seeing Tamara. And this caring attitude belonged to Tamara. Dahlia was just doing as Tamara had advised.

Slowly, he took his jacket back from Dahlia. "Let's talk."

"About the divorce? Please, I need more time..."

He shook his head in disagreement. "No, it's not about the divorce. Lately, we've been misunderstanding each other. About the job, I didn't mean you shouldn't take the job. I said it's going to be hard to combine a job with raising a kid. But if you think you can handle it, you can go ahead and take the job. But if you can't, I'll be responsible for you and my son."

"I understand you, but I've decided to take the job."

"Okay. Good. Congratulations on your job."

"Thanks," she said very softly. For a few second no one said anything.

Raymond cleared his throat. "Ahem! I think I'll go take a shower real quick."

"Yeah. You should. I'll serve dinner."

Raymond began to cautiously climb the stairs

that headed to the bedroom. Mid-way the stairs, he stopped and looked back at Dahlia. "Dahlia," he called, trying to even his voice. "You didn't like staying home. You didn't like not making any financial contribution in the house, but you didn't tell me. Why?"

"You've been talking to Tamara!" Dahlia said, almost yelling.

"Yeah. Obviously, you've been talking to her too. That's where you got your new polished attitude." He had said that and he wished he could take it back.

"Don't you dare insult me!"

"I'm sorry. I didn't mean to say that."

"What did you mean to say?" she asked, glaring at him. "Everything is about Tamara. You're asking for divorce because of Tamara."

"Do not bring Tamara into this," he snapped.

"Don't bring Tamara into this?" she asked, ice in her voice. "Tamara is in this already."

Raymond put his hand to his forehead. "Please, don't let us get into any argument again. Please."

"I know it's always about Tamara. You love her. And I get it. And I might never be able to be half the woman she is but I'm trying..."

He removed his hand from his forehead and looked at her. "Dahlia, you're getting it all wrong. This conversation is not about who I loved or who I love. I'm asking you why you didn't talk to me. Why you had to lie to people that I had problem with taking care of the responsibility alone. Why you didn't tell me that you don't like staying home without a job."

"Because you don't listen to me!"

"That's not true."

"Yes, it's true. Do you know how many times I wanted to talk to you but you were so far away? Your mind, the life in you was always somewhere else, with Tamara, I guess."

Now the woman was blaming him for everything, he thought.

"Look, Raymond, I know you didn't exactly plan for us to be married. But we are. And we are in this together. And you should at least try to love me."

"You did not make it easy to love you!" he barked.

"You didn't give me a chance! At all!" she yelled.

"I was trying so hard to love you. I wanted to be an honorable man. I wanted to love my wife, I wanted to be committed to my marriage. I gave you a chance, but you blew it when you cheated." He stopped to swallow. "On our bed. You didn't only cheat on me, you created a mess. A mess that I had to handle, that I had to get myself involved in and fix for you."

"What I did, it was wrong. It was bad. But please, forgive me. Take me back. Love me. And I wouldn't blow this chance again." Taking few steps closer to him, she tried to touch his chest.

Raymond drew back slightly.

Dahlia nodded very gently and kept her hands to herself.

"I'm sorry," Raymond said, walking past her

and heading for the door. He got into his car, cranked the key into the ignition and pulled onto the street.

****

Raymond knocked on Tamara's door. He had been knocking for almost two minutes and she didn't open. What the heck was he expecting by coming to her house? It was well past 9:00pm. He had stopped at the store to purchase a bottle of red wine and had also picked a couple of movies from Hollywood Videos. He wanted to enjoy a peaceful atmosphere and he couldn't think of anyone capable of creating that atmosphere except Tamara. He wanted to spend time with her. His heart lies with Tamara and she wouldn't even talk to him. She had been ignoring the feelings between them, treating him like a complete stranger.

For the last time, he knocked again and waited. And the door opened.

"What do you want?" Tamara asked, glaring at his face.

Raymond gave a sarcastic smile. "Hi. Hello. How are you doing?"

Tamara returned his sarcastic smile. "Hello. Hi. I'm doing fine. What do you want?"

"Someone skipped dinner at home and was thinking he could crash with you and get to eat dinner."

"And that someone is you. Right?"

"Kind of."

"Go home, Raymond. You're married. You're not supposed to be here. Go back to your wife."

She wanted to slam the door in his face, but Raymond stopped her before she could. "Oops, I forgot that you don't cook."

Sweeping her aside, he stepped into the house and walked toward the kitchen.

"Raymond!" Tamara called as she followed.

Getting to the kitchen, Raymond glanced around. "I'm right." His lips curved into a gentle smile. "You haven't changed one bit. You still don't cook. You don't even have any kitchen gadget."

Dropping the wine on the table, he looked at her. "Do you at least have two cups that we can use to drink this?"

"I may not cook. I may not have so many kitchen gadgets, but I have cups. And plates." She rolled her eyes at him. "And spoons."

"Good. Now, get the cups and let's drink this and enjoy the moment..."

Putting all her energy in to it, she cut him off and shouted, "Raymond!"

He stopped talking and looked at her. He could see the rise and fall of her chest. Her heart was beating fast.

"You shouldn't be here," she said, her voice went back to being calm and soft.

If Raymond was having any doubt before now, the doubt had disappeared. He was now certain that Tamara still felt something for him. Why else would she be breathing this hard? She was scared. Scared of being alone with him. Scared of what might happen between them. Scared of what had almost happened between them each time they were alone. He wanted to just grab her right there and make sweet, passionate love to her, but thought against it and said, "It's okay if you don't want us to use the cup. We'll just drink from the bottle."

"Raymond!"

"There's a Chinese restaurant newly opened not far from here. The food is good. Have you tried it?"

"Raymond, you should go home."

"I take that to mean no. I'll order some." He reached for his cell phone and made a call to the restaurant. "Nǐ hǎo," he said, meaning hello in Chinese. He had made a business trip to China so many times that he was able to learn a bit of the language.

"You don't have to show off your poor Chinese. They're called Chinese restaurant, that doesn't mean they don't speak English."

He pretended to be surprise, and then covered the mouthpiece of the phone. "Really? They speak English?"

She let out a breath of pretend exasperation.

Raymond smiled, walking over to the living room as he continued to order for the food. By the time he finished placing the order, Tamara already joined him in the living room. "Our order will be here soon. We could start watching the movie while we wait."

He went to the DVD Player and played one of the movies he had brought with him. He relaxed himself on the couch as The Dictator started playing. Tamara stood opposite of him, still trying to make him leave. But he knew he wasn't going nowhere. Maybe after the movie, after the dinner and after spending a nice time with the woman he loved, then he might think of leaving.

"Come here," he said softly but firmly, and patted the couch next to him.

She hesitated.

"Mara... come HERE," he said firmly with a sexy voice, in a tone of voice that refused to be denied.

Very slowly, she walked over to the couch and sat down beside him...though several feet away as if she was afraid of being very close to him. Raymond smiled gently and ignored her unnecessary cautiousness. Even though sitting close to her had caused a tingle in his manhood and he could feel it rise to occasion, he resisted the temptation.

Ten minutes into the movie, they were laughing easily together without embarrassment. The gap between them had closed up a bit.

Tamara laughed hard, got carried away and rested her head on his chest. Wrapping his hand around her waist, Raymond pulled her closer. And she didn't resist. Finally, the intimacy he had craved for. The moment he had waited for.

A light knock on the door cut short the moment. Bad timing, Raymond made a low angry grunt.

"I'll get it." He stood, walked over to the door to receive the order. Handling one box of hibachi rice to Tamara, he settled beside her too.

Tamara opened the box and ate. "Mmm. This is delicious."

Raymond smiled. "Told ya."

She ate two to three spoons and looked at Raymond, smiling. "I like the food. How come I didn't know about this Chinese Restaurant and its right here in my neighborhood?"

Picking an octopus from his meal, he held it closer to her mouth. "Here, have a taste of this."

Tamara drew back slightly and hesitated, squeezing her face to express her disgust.

"C'mon! Try it. It's tasty. You're going to like it."

Tamara relaxed and he fed her the octopus.

Her face wrinkled as she chewed the little octopus. "It's too spicy!"

Breathing hard, she opened her mouth and blew some air into it with her palm.

Raymond laughed. Reaching for the red wine, he opened it quickly and gave it to her. She drank from the bottle. And when she felt better, she made her palm into a fist and playfully hit him by the shoulder.

Raymond laughed and pulled her closer, noting that her countenance seemed to soften and her smile genuine. They finished eating and their concentration went back to The Dictator.

They laughed together and Raymond's hand took up permanent position around her waist, the distinctive and delicious scent of her overcoming the smell of hibachi rice and humanity around him.

"You want more wine?" he asked.

She leaned closer enough to make sure he could see her warning look. "This isn't a date, Raymond."

He grinned and gave her a sideway glance. "Fake it for me. Okay?"

Raymond felt his touch sent vibrations through her. She gave him a sidelong glance, eyeing him with suspicion. "And just what are you doing?"

His gaze locked on hers, very warm and loving. "I told you once. I'm wooing you back to my arms."

She didn't give a response and she didn't move away from him.

Maybe it was the clean, fruity fragrance of her hair, or the feel of her slender arm wrapped around him. Or maybe it was the intense connection he felt with this woman. Only her. He hadn't felt it with any woman in his entire life. He didn't really know what the hell it was, but he felt like…

"I'm at a distinct disadvantage," he softly announced, so close to her ear that he could feel her shuddered at the vibration his voice had created. "You know a lot about me than I know about you since the breakup."

"What do you want to know?"

"Do you have a boyfriend?"

"No."

"Why?"

"Because…because…."

She couldn't finish the statement. And even

though she didn't say a thing, he knew why she couldn't move on after he left.

"I'm sorry," he said very gently. "I'm very very sorry."

She kept looking in his eyes. She swallowed, her lips parting slightly.

Face to face, as though it were the most natural thing in the world, he wrapped his arms around her waist and she placed her hands on his chest. With her gazing up at him with the apology accepted kind of look, he just had to dip his head about two inches...open his mouth to meet hers and...

He kissed her.

She tasted like salt and wine. Her lips were warm and inviting and when they opened to him, he flicked his tongue against the roof of her mouth. His head buzzed with the instant pleasure and he held his arms more tightly around her, angling his head to make the kiss more intense and longer.

And it lasted long enough to send fire through his veins.

Very slowly, she pulled away. Her eyes lightly closed and her lips curved into a slow gentle smile. For some reason, that made him relieved and pleased him more than anything. She hadn't yanked away and slapped him hard across his face like the previous time he had kissed her. Instead, she looked like she enjoyed being kissed by him.

He wasn't expecting it, but she lifted her face toward him again and initiated the kiss. A billion clashing emotions rushed through him, but he had them under control.

He tilted his head to taste more of her, caressing her beautiful hair. He felt himself stir into hardness as the flare of desire burnt through him.

Slowly, his hands went to her breast, cupping it in his palm. Under his palm, her heart raced just like his. Her breathing was rapid, just like his. And he could swear that her body was fully aroused...just like his.

Again, she pulled away very slowly. This time, she didn't look at him. She swallowed hard and said, "Good night, Raymond."

And he knew better than to argue with her or try to overstay his welcome.

Chapter 7

Making out with Raymond Brock had been foolish. And unbelievable.

Okay, it had been unbelievably foolish.

But Tamara had been so turned on by him. Maybe because he knew her so well. He hadn't even forgotten how much she hated cooking. He had her when he walked right into her kitchen and said *you haven't changed one bit. You still don't cook. You don't even have any kitchen gadget.*

He had her right there. Truth be told, she'd wanted to kiss him. She wanted to kiss him again. But she knew kissing Raymond again would be disastrous and wouldn't end well.

Her thoughts were cut short as Drake, Sherry and Megan walked toward her.

"Hey, Drake," she said in greeting.

"Is that how you greet the best attorney in the building?" Drake said with an arrogant smile.

"I don't know where you got that idea from, but because some people have been kissing your ass doesn't make you the best attorney in the building," Tamara replied.

He roared with laughter. "I don't know about other people kissing my ass, but..." he paused a little, cast a look at Tamara's backside and licked his lower lip. "I wouldn't mind kissing somebody else's."

Tamara glanced at Sherry and Megan. "Any of you have a gun? I need to shoot this guy in the head."

He gave his *I'm going to do whatever I want and get away with it* kind of smile. "That would be great. You'd send me from heaven to heaven."

Tamara raised a brow. "From which heaven to which heaven?"

He winked at her. "The heaven between your legs to the Lord's heaven."

"What? I think I should sue you for sexual harassment."

He smiled again. "By definition, sexual harassment is unwanted sexual advances."

"Are you saying that I want your sexual advances? Hell no!"

"Look, you're even smiling as you say the Hell no. It tells me you love my advances. But you have nothing to worry about. When I ask you out for dinner or buy you a rose, then you should worry."

"You like women!" Sherry yelled.

"Oh Yeah! You can say that again," Tamara confirmed. "In college, he was so famous for being a Casanova that his name became synonymous to the word 'screw'." She used her hands to do the quote and unquote sign. "So instead of saying he screwed the girl last night, you'll say he draked the girl last night."

"With that kind of reputation, women should be flooding this office. How come I haven't seen any woman around him since I've been here?" Sherry asked.

"That's because he has changed. I haven't seen him with a woman in more than one year. Sweet Lord! I wonder how he's coping," Tamara replied.

Drake laughed.

"Enough of this!" Megan yelled. "Can we go ahead and start the day's work?"

"Someone is angry because I'm not flirting with her," Drake replied.

Megan glared at him.

"Drake, Megan is right," Tamara said. "This is an office. I'm not saying you should stop flirting, but, please, tone it down a bit."

"Yes, boss."

"So where are we on the Brock's case?" Tamara asked.

"I followed Dahlia throughout last week," Sherry began. "Her routine is simple. She takes her son to daycare every morning, and then she goes to work at your mom's store and from there she goes straight home after work. She purchases groceries every Wednesdays and on Friday she made a stop at a jewelry store where she purchased a male wristwatch. I talked to her about it and she said their wedding anniversary is coming up and it's a gift for her husband."

Tamara sighed.

"I followed Raymond," Drake began. "He goes

to work every morning. On Wednesdays, he drops his suit off at the drycleaner's place before going to work and he picks it back when coming back from work. Basketball after work on Thursday. Most of his time in office is spent with his personal assistant, Anita. But Anita is married and from my findings, she isn't the kind of woman that would have an affair."

Tamara sighed again.

"Now we can trust that none of them is having an affair," Sherry said.

For a split second, no one said a thing.

Megan broke the silence. "Dahlia called the office this morning. She said to thank you for the positive changes in her marriage. She said, recently, she and her husband have been having a heart to heart conversation, better than before."

Tamara nodded. "We need to move to the next step. Megan!" she called. "I want you to schedule Mr. & Mrs. Brock for an appointment. It's time to bring them together and talk to them."

"Okay," Megan replied.

"So this is the point where we schedule them for therapy, right?" Sherry asked.

"No," Drake replied. "Therapy is for couples trying to make their marriage work. It's not therapy. Just see it as Tamara inviting the couples to talk some sense into them."

Tamara was quiet for a micro second and then she looked at Sherry and gave a gentle smile. "Sherry, would you please help me order some kitchen utensils and have it delivered at my house."

"You got to be kidding me. I'm an intern. I'm supposed to be getting experience on Legal studies."

Tamara smiled again. "Thank you, Sherry. I'll be expecting my order." When Megan and Sherry had gone, Tamara turned to Drake. "Drake, you think you could press some buttons and get me the Brock's bank account statement?"

"Sure. I can do that."

"Okay. Please, get their bank account and credit card statements."

"Yes, boss."

He started to walk away and had only taken two to three steps when Tamara stopped him.

"Drake," she called. "I know that you knew Raymond had been meeting with me. Thank you...you know...for not spilling the beans in the presence of everybody."

"Don't worry about it. That's what friends do. They got each other's back. I've got your back, Tamara."

Tamara nodded and smiled.

"Tamara, my advice as a friend, please, stay away from Raymond. Old feelings die hard."

Tamara felt as if she had received a punch. The truth in Drake's words cut through her heart. He was damn right. She needed to stay away from Raymond, or else...

****

"Tamara Price?"

Tamara nodded proudly, fully aware of the weight the name carried.

"Tamara...please, you have... to help me," the woman said. Her words broke off as chunks between gasping breaths. Her eyes were red and puffy. Tamara need not be told that the woman had been crying and that she had been a victim in her marriage.

Tamara's heart went out to her and she stood from her armchair and walked toward the woman. "Welcome to Tamara Price and Associates," she said, and then picked her desk phone. "We have a new client!"

Few seconds later, Drake, Megan and Sherry walked into her office. When they all settled into their chair, she turned to the woman. "You're going to tell us who you are, what happened in your marriage and how you want us to help you."

She tried to say something, but before she could, tears rolled speedily down her cheeks. Megan handed her a handkerchief while Tamara folded her arms, listening intently to her.

"My name is Linda Shepherd," she began.

"Wife of Bishop Shepherd, the famous preacher?" Megan questioned.

She nodded, still wiping her tears.

"Even Bishop Shepherd doesn't have a perfect marriage," Drake said and broke out into a loud laugh.

Tamara shot him a glare.

"C'mon, Tamara, where's your sense of humor?" he questioned, still laughing while everyone remained stony.

Drake had a weird sense of humor, Tamara had always known that. She turned to Linda and said, "Please, ignore him."

Linda nodded and began gently. "My husband beat me…" She broke out into a loud sob.

Tamara unfolded her arms and placed a hand on her shoulder to console her. "How many times?"

She stared back at Tamara. "I can't count. Many times since we got married about 10 years ago."

"What!" Sherry exclaimed. "Can we just sue him for battery already?"

"No. We can't," Drake replied.

"All men are the same. Men are beasts!" Sherry said, anger flaring in her eyes.

"That's bias and unfair!" Drake countered.

Megan looked Linda in the face, jabbing a finger on the table. "If he hits you once, he's going to do it again. And again. And again. So it is better if you get out of this marriage as quick as possible."

"Enough!" Tamara yelled. She wondered when they will all learn to put emotions aside. They needed to learn to stop letting their emotions get in the way of their job.

The glare she shot them felt like scolding and they all kept mute.

Withdrawing her glare, she turned to Linda and began, softening her voice. "Linda, I want you to tell me how you want me to help you. Do you want me to get you a divorce or you want me to help you save your marriage?"

Linda stared at Tamara a while and then her gaze dropped. "I don't know," she said amidst sobs.

"Linda, you have to know. I can't make the decision for you. It has to be your decision." She paused, waiting for her to give a response. When she didn't say anything, Tamara asked her again. This time, her voice was louder and she emphasized every word. "Do you want me to get you a divorce or you want me to help save your marriage?"

Sherry yelled it out. "I want to save my marriage!"

"Good!" She looked at Megan. "Megan, I want you to prepare the petition for dissolution of marriage and let Linda have her husband sign it."

Linda raised a brow in disbelief. "I said I want to save my marriage." She stared at Megan, Sherry and then Drake. They all looked confused as she. And then she looked back at Tamara. "I don't want a divorce."

"I know. We just need to make your husband think you really want a divorce. We need to place the consequences of his actions before him."

"Still. Whatever the intentions are, divorce is not what I want. I love my husband. I still do." She dropped her head gently. "It's my fault. Maybe if I can show him more love, maybe he will change. It's my fault."

Tamara sat on the table and faced Linda, looking her directly in the eye. "Linda, look at me." Her voice came very gentle. "It's not your fault. For 10 years, you've done everything. You've endured him and loved him and there's nothing you could have done more. And that was why you came to me. And trust me, I can help you. I want to help you save your marriage. Let me help you and I promise you that you won't get divorced. We just need your husband to believe that you are capable of it. Look, one of the reasons your husband kept doing that to you was because he knows how much you love him. If you can show him that the love you have for him doesn't stop you from getting a divorce if he doesn't stop hitting you, I believe he will change."

"You think so?"

Tamara shook his head. "I don't think so. I know so."

Linda shook her head gently in agreement.

"Good." Tamara turned to Megan. "Prepare the petition for dissolution of marriage."

"Okay."

"Drake," Tamara called. "Do some digging on Bishop Shepherd. I want to know what his life is like. Information on his past, before he became the preacher, would be most helpful."

"Yes, boss."

"Sherry," she called. "Work with Drake."

Sherry smiled in excitement. "Great!"

As Drake walked toward the door and Sherry followed, Tamara peered at the both of them and then she called, "Drake!" Her voice was harsher than she had intended.

"The way you Drake me all over the place, I'm gonna think you're in love with me," he replied.

Tamara gave a mischievous smile. "Remember, you're not allowed to screw a colleague."

"Oh! You mean, Sherry?" He shook his head playfully. "Not my taste. And for the record, she isn't my colleague. I'm her boss, she's a baby lawyer!"

Sherry glared at him. "I'm not a baby lawyer!"

"You're right," he replied. "You're a little less than a baby lawyer!"

Sherry made her palm into a fist to playfully hit Drake. Drake dodged her fist and ran. Sherry ran after him.

They looked good together, Tamara said to herself as she watched them ran out of the office.

Chapter 8

Tamara Price had always considered herself cool under pressure, but she was losing all coolness as she waited in her office for the Brocks. She was supposed to talk to them about how to survive the troubles in their marriage, but she didn't think she was capable of it. She hadn't met the two traitors together. The friend who took her man. The man who betrayed her. How on earth was she supposed to counsel these traitors about not getting divorced when, truly, all she wanted was for them to get divorced and rot in hell.

Trying to concentrate, she told herself that the Brocks were just another client. Nothing more. Nothing less. She tried to think about what to say to the couples. Her imagination brought Dahlia into her office with Raymond. And then she imagined herself standing before Dahlia, face close, eyes locked together. And in the scariest tone she could come up with, she yelled, "Get the hell out of my office, bitch! You stole my man!"

Quickly, she shook her head and dismissed the imagination. That wouldn't work. It was completely unprofessional.

Again she tried to imagine the situation. Her imagination brought Dahlia and Raymond into her office. With a professional smile, she extended a palm in greeting. She felt her stomach melted as Raymond's hand caught hers. Air blew the scent of his cologne into her nostrils and she felt tempted to lean closer. She did and from there, it happened naturally. She kissed him. Right there in the presence of his wife—Dahlia.

Quickly, she shook her head again to dismiss the images. That was worse! Was unethical! Was unprofessional! Frustrated, she placed her head on the table.

Few seconds later, she heard a slight knock on the door. By the time she raised her head, her eyes fell on Dahlia and Raymond as they both walked into her office. She concentrated her gaze on Raymond. He looked exactly the same in her imaginations. He was wearing a navy suit over a white shirt and dark blue tie, exactly what he wore in her imaginations.

It could only mean one thing. Everything was going to happen the same way she had imagined it. She had kissed him back the other night. And she knew she was capable of doing it again. Fear took over her sense of self and she began to panic.

"Miss Price..." Raymond said.

Before he could say further, Tamara cut him off. "Excuse me," she said, her voice shaky. "One minute, please."

Very quickly, she ran to the restroom. When she entered the restroom and was sure she was alone, she began to pace back and forth, doing this thing with her hands that she does when she panics. She flapped them frantically, like she was stuffy and was trying to blow some air with her hands. She realized she actually felt stuffy. Very fast, she unbuttoned her shirt for more air, exposing her breast cupped in a laced bra.

She was at a loss on what to do. Quickly, she took her cell phone from the pocket of her pants and placed a call.

"Hello, Drake," she said.

"Let me guess. By now, you are in the restroom, almost naked, pacing back and forth and flapping your hands like a drowning bird."

"What? Well yeah. How do you know that? Have you been spying on me?"

Tamara heard him stifled a laugh. "No. But I saw you do that back then in high school when you were going for your first date."

She transferred her cell phone to the left while she continued flapping her right hand. "High school is a long time ago. I should stop doing this. I'm a grown woman."

"As you can see, you didn't do much of growing up since high school."

"Drake, but this is isn't a date. Why the hell am I panicking?"

"Because it's Raymond. He betrayed you. And you have to talk him out of divorcing his wife. Because you still love him and..."

She cut him off. "Yeah, yeah, yeah, I get it. But I can't do this. Get your ass over here and come do the counseling, the talking or whatever!"

"Yes, you can do it. You're good at it. It's what you do and you do it better than anyone else. Just breathe in and breathe out and you'll be fine. Bye."

"Drake! Drake! Don't you dare hang up! Drake!"

When she heard no response, she dropped the phone. *Son of a bitch!* She muttered under her breath.

She decided to take his advice. Quickly, she buttoned her shirt, check her makeup, shut her eyes and breathe in and out slowly. And then she sashayed confidently back into her office.

"Mr. & Mrs. Brock, I'm so sorry for the delay."

"That's okay," Dahlia replied.

Tamara extended a hand in greeting. "Welcome to Tamara Price & Associates."

Afterward, she took a seat. "Let's get down to business. First, I'd like to remind you that I'm not a marriage counselor. I'm just someone trying to help you get through this troubled time and talk you out of getting a divorce. In the end if I think your marriage is beyond saving, I'd recommend a divorce."

They nodded in understanding.

"Good." She opened the folder on her table and glanced through it very quickly. "Having studied your case, I decided this wouldn't be a question and answer section. I want you to pretend as if I'm not seated here and just go ahead and discuss the issue."

"What?" Raymond replied. "We can't discuss as if you're not here and..."

"Honey," Dahlia said, her voice very gentle. "You promise to do everything she asks of us."

The way she said "honey" caused an irritation in Tamara's stomach. Bitch! She had the guts to call him honey in her presence.

Tamara knew she was being too bitter, but she couldn't help it.

"Okay. I agree. How do we start?" Raymond asked.

"You can start by telling her why you want a divorce. From my conversation with her, she doesn't seem to know."

"Of course, she knows."

Tamara glanced at Dahlia. She didn't react to what Raymond said.

"Alright, Dahlia," Tamara said. "Maybe you should tell him why you don't want a divorce."

"Because I love you," Dahlia said, staring intently into Raymond's eyes.

Raymond chuckled. "What you did, if you love someone, do you do that to them?"

"I made a mistake. And I regret it very deeply. I'm sorry. Forgive me and let's start over."

"I can't. I can't forgive it. You think that makes me a terrible person?"

Tears filled Dahlia's eyes and she tried to blink it away. "Yes," she replied.

"I'm sorry." Raymond stood up and walked toward the door.

"Raymond!" Dahlia called. "Please, let's make this work. Raymond!" When Raymond didn't stop, she turned to Tamara. "Please, stop him."

"Let him leave. You, on the other hand, need

to start talking to me. What are you hiding from me? What did you do that's making him ask for a divorce?"

Her voice was harsher than she had intended it to be. She was angry. Angry because the look on Raymond's face indicated that he was hurt. Had always been hurting. And somehow, Dahlia was the one hurting him.

"I told you. He's asking for a divorce because I depended too much on him. I spent his money on unnecessary things. Now that I got a job and making some money of my own, I thought everything would be alright between us."

"Look at me, Dahlia. I am not a fool. If I find out that you are lying to me, if I find out that you are not telling the truth, I'll take my hands off your case. So for the last time, are you lying to me? Have you told me everything?"

Tears in her voice, Dahlia replied, "Yes, I told you everything."

Tamara nodded. "Okay. Go ahead and wait for me at the conference room. I'll see you in ten minutes."

Tamara reached for her desk phone and dialed. "Guys, I need you in my office now! We have to conclude on the Brock's case!"

Few minutes later, they were in her office. Tamara stood up, folded her arms and pacing back and forth. It was silent for some seconds. And then she broke the silence and turned to Drake. "Drake, did you get the Brocks' credit card statement that I asked of you?"

"Wait," Sherry said. "You ordered for their

credit card statement? I thought we agreed that the Brocks aren't hiding anything."

"Yes, boss. I got it," Drake replied, ignoring Sherry's comment. He pulled a document out of the folder in his hands and handed it to Tamara.

Tamara took the document and began to read through.

"At least, tell us what happened at the talk section with the Brocks," Megan said.

"Oh! That! It lasted for two minutes," she began, without taking her eyes off the document. "Mr. Brock is asking for a divorce because of something that his wife did to him. Something so big that he can't forgive. Something he can't tell me and something that Dahlia can't..." She stopped suddenly, took her eyes off the document and looked frantically at Drake. "Who is Steve Ryder?"

Drake raised a brow. "Really? I told you Steve Ryder is their gardener."

"Well, from the look of things, he is more than a gardener. First, it was Dahlia making too much phone calls to this person. And then Raymond paid him $50,000."

Drake nodded. "Obviously, you don't pay someone $50,000 to cut grasses and flowers."

Sherry asked, "Why all these suspicions for crying out loud. This couple isn't cheating. She even got her husband an expensive wristwatch for their upcoming anniversary."

"Hold on!" Tamara interrupted. "That transaction is not on their credit card statement," she said, reading through the statements again.

"That's because she paid with cash. It's a surprise gift, that's why she didn't want it showing on their credit card statement."

Tamara gave a knowing smile. "When your anniversary is coming up, even if it's a surprise gift, you usually don't bother about the transaction showing up on your credit card statement. Unless, of course, if the gift is not for your husband."

They stared at her skeptically.

Megan asked, "What are you trying to say?"

Tamara turned to Drake. "How old is Steve Ryder?"

Drake lifted an arm in a shrug. "About 16 or 17 years old."

Tamara sucked in her breath and gritted her teeth. "Bitch!" she said through clenched teeth.

Grabbing the document, she raced out of the office toward the conference room—where Dahlia had been waiting.

Chapter 9

"You lied to me!"

Tamara roared as she flung open the door and stood boldly in front of Dahlia while Drake, Megan and Sherry stood behind Tamara.

Eyebrows knitted close together in thought, Dahlia looked at Tamara. "I don't understand what you're talking about."

Tamara threw the document on the table before Dahlia and then folded her arms. "Who is Steve Ryder?"

Glancing at the document, Dahlia said, "This is our credit card statement."

"Who is Steve Ryder?" Tamara asked again, frowning.

"Our gardener."

"And why did Raymond pay him $50, 000?"

"Probably business...I don't know."

Tamara released her folded arm. "No, no, no. Don't tell me you don't know because I know you know." Tapping her fingers on the table, she glared at Dahlia. "You! Dahlia, you were screwing your gardener. You slept with Steve Ryder. And when your dirty secret came out to the open, the family threatened to sue you, because Steve is in fact a minor. Raymond had to come to your rescue. Although he was hurt that you cheated on him, he rescued you. He shut down the case by paying off Steve Ryder. He paid him $50,000 to shut him up. Raymond couldn't tell anyone the reason he wants a divorce because he is still covering your mess."

Close to tears, Dahlia glanced back at Tamara. "This is not true. None of this is true. Believe me, Tamara. I didn't sleep with Steve. Even if I did, no one can sue me because the age of consent for sex in Maryland is 16. And Steve is 17."

"Don't you dare throw the law at me. I studied the law. I know the law. Maryland's age of consent law applies differently if the older partner is in a position of trust or authority over the younger partner. This might be teachers, coaches and EMPLOYERS. In such cases, the age of consent is 18, or even 21."

For the next few seconds, no one said anything. Silence covered the room.

Finally, Dahlia said something. "Let's talk about this alone. Tell them to give us the room."

Tamara glanced at them. "You mean them?" she asked, pointing to Drake, Megan and Sherry.

Dahlia nodded.

"They are staying. They are not leaving. Whatever you got to say, say it now. They are the witness!"

Dahlia lowered her head gently. By the time

she would lift up her face, tears were rolling down her cheeks. "After I had my baby, I felt as if I had lost my youthfulness. Steve. He came around and made me feel younger. I felt seventeen. Before I knew it, I was carried away and I made the greatest mistake of my life. It was a mistake."

"Mistake? You are 32 years old and you're screwing your employee who is a minor. A 17 years old boy!"

"Don't judge me, Tamara. Don't judge me."

Tamara shook her head. "No, no. I am not judging you. That's not the issue. The issue is that you lied to me. If you had told me from the start, I would have handled your case differently. I would have appeal to Raymond and made him understand that no one is perfect instead of attacking him like I did."

"I'm sorry. Steve was a mistake. I made a mistake. It was a one-time thing."

"Don't tell me another lie, Dahlia. It wasn't a one-time thing. You had an affair with him."

"I'm not lying. It was a one-time thing. Why would I choose Steve over my husband? Raymond is everything. He is man enough. He is the love of my life. He is worth billions. He is the father of my son."

Eyebrows knitted close together, Tamara glanced sharply at Dahlia. "Did you just say he is worth billions? How did you know that?"

Dahlia didn't respond.

Tamara narrowed her gaze as if doing so would help her read Dahlia's mind. "His job as a journalist can't make him a billionaire. Unless if you know that he...is..."

Dahlia interrupted. "The illegitimate son of James Connor, the billionaire." She wiped her tears and a knowing grin covered her face. "I also know his inheritance is worth billions."

Tamara's butt slowly found the armchair. A small sigh escape through her lips. It was a secret. No one was supposed to know that Raymond Brock was the illegitimate son of James Connor. Tamara only got to know because she had represented Raymond as his attorney when the mess had started.

Actually, the real mess started about 35 years ago when a maid, Rachel Brock, was impregnated by her Mr. Billionaire Perfect boss. Of course, the billionaire denied having anything to do with the maid, and threatened her never to speak of their affair to anyone. Rachel gave birth to a baby boy. A boy without a father. A boy who was born a Connor, but was never raised as a Connor. That boy was Raymond Brock.

Thirty years later, the billionaire, while on his sick bed, decided it was time to meet his son. He met his son briefly before he died. After his death, it was discovered that the billionaire made a will and left everything for his eldest son— Raymond Brock. The two legitimate sons— not willing to let go of their inheritance— started a war. A war Tamara had to get involve because she was Raymond's fiancée and attorney. She fought the battle and won. In the end, they arrived at a fair deal. Raymond would get his inheritance, would become the CEO of Connor Corp, if he agreed not to go public about his relationship with James Connor. It wasn't a difficult thing to do because Raymond wanted a normal life. He didn't want to take a last name that would take his normal life from him. He didn't want to form an alliance or a relationship that would make people think they had to impress him, get in his good grace or win him over.

Raymond Brock took the deal. And while people knew him as the face on Television and a shareholder at Connor Corp, he was in fact the man sitting on the big chair of Connor Corp. And the few people who knew the truth? Tamara paid them off and told them to take the secret to their grave. But, in this world, nothing stays a secret forever. Obviously, someone had leaked the secret and Dahlia had found out. Tamara wondered how many more people knew about the big secret.

Tamara let out a deep breath. "You know the big secret. What's your game plan?"

Dahlia rested her hands on the table and while leaning closer, she said, "Tamara, for me it's all about the money. I want you to join me. Let's do this together."

"You don't need me. Raymond already asked for a divorce. Take the divorce and you can get quite a lot of money. You both didn't have a prenup in place, anyways."

"You see, it's not that easy. I'm going to divorce Raymond, but not now. He's going to divorce me on the grounds of infidelity and that's not good for me. You're a lawyer. You know what I'm talking about."

Tamara shook her head. "No. I didn't quite follow."

Dahlia hesitated a little while, and then she continued, "Join me. Help me to stay married to Raymond for a little longer."

Tamara tried to put herself in Dahlia's shoes. She tried to think in the way Dahlia would think. *If I love money and I married my husband for money, she thought. I should be happy that he is asking for divorce because I can get 50% of his wealth. Why would I throw away the 50% to stay married to him when I didn't quite love him? Unless if I have my eyes on the 100%. The whole assets could be mine if he was dead or...*

Tamara scowled. "Are you by chance planning to harm Raymond?"

"Join me," she whispered and leaned closer. "With your legal knowledge, we will get away with it."

Tamara shot her a deadly glare. "Joining you is not happening?"

"We will get away with it. Our lives will be better. We won't have to worry about money. Ever again!"

Tamara's glare deepened. "I won't let you hurt Raymond."

"Why are you on his side? He doesn't deserve your loyalty or protection. He has no respect for you."

Tamara shook her head. "That's not true."

"After everything you did for him, he betrayed

you. He cast you aside without a moment of thought."

Tamara slowly shook her head again. "That doesn't matter."

"But it must have hurt so much when he left you. It must hurt to be overlooked and betrayed that much when you have the ability to destroy him."

Too close to tears to speak, she swallowed. "That's the way it has to be."

"Tamara, it doesn't have to be that way. Men are not worth it. You can get your revenge on him. You can finally be at peace with yourself. You can finally be happy."

"I don't have to be happy."

"So be it!" Dahlia stood up and leaned closer, face closed, and eyes locked together. "If you refuse to join me, then stay away from me and my husband. If you get in my way, I will destroy everything you love most in this world. Raymond and your job. I will ruin you and no one will be able to fix you." She reached for her purse and began to walk away. After two steps, she stopped and glanced back at Tamara. "I know that you and Raymond have been seeing each other. If you don't stay away, I'll go to the press and announce that the marriage fixer is sleeping with my husband, ruining my marriage instead of fixing it."

Dahlia got to the door and Drake step aside for her. Before she could open the door, Tamara called, "Dahlia," she said, anger in her voice. "You've just started a battle and I'm fighting on the side of Raymond." She stood up and walked closer to Dahlia. Lips tightened in anger, she glared at her. "I do not care if you destroy my reputation, but if you so much as hurt Raymond or even pull a strand of hair from his body, I will track you down. I will hunt you and I will rain down a godly lake that burns with fire and brimstone upon you. I will fight you and your entire family with the law. And by the time I'm done with you, you are going to regret the rest of your wasted life. Know that these are not empty threats. I'm not bluffing. You know what I'm capable of. So my advice to you, you better run. Because whether or not you hurt Raymond, I'm going to destroy you for taking Raymond away from me. But that is just an advice, one you can choose to disregard at your own peril."

Chapter 10

Tamara Price's day was getting worse by the minute.

The weather had been fine when she left work that evening, but then all of a sudden cloud gathered and great sheets of water started pouring out of the dark skies. By the time she'd reached home, she could barely see the road. The fogged windshield offered no chance for a good vision and the trip took thirty minutes longer than normal.

Annoyance painted Tamara Price's expression as she parked in her garage and got out of the car. Hours earlier, she'd been upset when she discovered Dahlia's plan was to stay married to Raymond, hurt him or even murder him and make away with his wealth. In the wake of the discovery, she had been so angry that she threatened Dahlia. The thought that Raymond could die by the hands of Dahlia had drove her mad. And she had threatened to do things she might not be capable of.

Again, she wondered why she chose to fight on

the side of Raymond. The man had hurt her more than anyone she had ever known. The man had showed her love and then exposed her to the harsh reality of the other side of love. He had run off to Paris to get married to her best friend. He didn't even tell her what she did wrong. He didn't break up with her. He just ran off to Paris to marry Dahlia. And even though it had been a year since the incident, it still hurt as if it was yesterday. Each day, the pain in her heart had deepened. The man had hurt her too much, so what was she doing fighting for him, protecting him, and more importantly why did she care so much about him that she threatened to destroy his enemy. Because you still love him, you idiot.

Grabbing an umbrella, she stepped out of the car. As she struggled with opening up the umbrella, the intensity of the wind increased and before she knew it her umbrella was gone. Damn! Her hair was going to be wet. Reflexively, she placed her purse over her head.

Glancing around in the near darkness, she tried to look for her umbrella which the wind had taken from her. She was still looking when she saw lightning struck from the dark sky. And then she heard the deafening sound of thunder.

Tamara shuddered.

The thunder and lightning was so intense. Almost as if Zeus was in rage and had struck the earth with another lightning bolt.

Screw the umbrella!

With the purse still over her head, Tamara started running toward the house. She had almost run into the porch when she felt her leg hit something. She stopped to see what it was, but the near darkness offered no chance for a view. So she stooped over to touch and have a feel of what it was. It felt like it was package.

She didn't remember ordering for anything. What was a package doing in front of her house? She touched again.

Right about then, she remembered she had asked Sherry to help order some kitchen utensils.

The package was actually hers and she couldn't leave it just lying there in the rain. It would have been better if the delivery man had at least dropped the package in the porch.

She removed the purse from her head, placed it on the package and bent down to pick up the package.

Damn! Did it have to be this heavy?

She tried again the second time. Failed.

Suddenly she felt a covering over her head. She looked up to see what it was.

"Hi," he said as he held the umbrella over her head.

Tamara didn't have to be to be told who it was. She would recognize the voice even in her sleep. She looked back and her eyes caught his frame. Raymond Brock. She was right.

"Hold the umbrella and let me help you with that," he said.

Could it get any worse? One, her day had been ruined by the knowledge of Dahlia's evil plot. Two, the stupid rain had ruined everything including her hair and she might need to flat iron the hair before going to work tomorrow morning. And three, that man, Raymond, was standing next to her on a day like this— a day she was feeling helpless. And by offering to help, he was making her feel as if she really was helpless, couldn't do anything on her own. Could it really get any worse?

"No, but thanks," she replied. Her voice was loud by necessity to be heard over the rain and the wind whipping through her damp hair and clothes.

"MARA," he growled. "Don't be stubborn. And unreasonable. Let me help you. You're wet, cold and shivering and there's no way you can carry that on your own."

Tamara was drenched and she was shivering. She knew that she needed help.

But not from him.

The man had called her his heartbeat, told her he couldn't live without her and the next minute he had run off to Paris to marry her best friend. Such a fool she'd been to have believed him. And even though, he had apologized to her the other day that they had dinner in her place, still she couldn't forget the pain. Apology couldn't take away the memory, couldn't take away the pain.

But she was smarter now. She was going to be his divorce attorney. She would protect him from Dahlia if need be. But never again would she let him play Mr. Nice Guy and crawl back into her heart. Well, he never left your heart, you idiot. The kiss they had shared the other night was a proof of that.

Instead of giving him the rude response, she said calmly, "I don't need your help. I've been fine on my own. I am fine on my own."

Without waiting for a response, she bent over to lift the package but the box torn. It wasn't surprising. The box was soaked. Thank goodness, the utensils were neatly packed into a plastic bag.

Summoning all her strength, she lifted the bag and began to walk to the house. She hadn't taken more than two steps when one of her feet slipped on the slippery pavement and she completely lost her balance.

She fell down in an ungainly sprawl. As she tried to catch herself, one of her ankles twisted beneath her.

At that moment, the only thing she could think of— as unreasonable as she knew it to be— was that this whole mess was Raymond's fault. If she didn't have to spend her evening trying to talk him and his wife out of getting a divorce, if she didn't waste so much time trying to find out Dahlia's evil plot, she would have been home before the stupid rain even started.

Without prior warning, strong hands started hauling her up.

Startled and disoriented, she fought them reflexively.

"Dammit it, Mara," Raymond said between gritted teeth, leaning over again to get a better grip on her waist so he could pull her up. "Why are you so stubborn? What are you trying to prove?"

"That I do not need your help," she yelled, pushing his hands away.

Slowly, Raymond let go of her.

Even if she lacked strength, she certainly had enough pride to walk into her house—while carrying a package that weighed 40 pounds— on a twisted ankle.

She stood up. Leaning on one leg, she lifted the package. And then in her attempt to walk, her weight landed on the hurting foot and then she fell. Again.

A moan of despair escaped through her lips.

It hurt so much that she thought she might cry.

Raymond walked closer to her, crouched and looked into her eyes. Tamara could see the pity in his eyes even in the near darkness.

With a very gentle voice, he began, "What do you want to do? You don't want to accept my help?"

Tears rolled down her cheeks. The rain quickly washed it away, but she knew Raymond could still see her tears.

Slowly, she held Raymond's hand. Amidst tears, she said, "please. Help me," she pleaded, avoiding his gaze.

Raymond leaned closer. Arm around her, he got a grip on her waist and pulled her up. Letting go of the umbrella, he put his arms beneath her, lifted her up like a baby and as gently as he was able he carried her and walked to the house.

Chapter 11

When Raymond got to the door, he remembered he didn't have the key to the house.

Raymond asked, "Where's your key?"

"In my purse," she replied.

At that point, Raymond realized the purse must have fallen out there in the rain. Ever so gently, she placed her down and let her sit on the floor of the porch. And then he rushed back to get her purse and the package.

He was drenched and cold. But that didn't matter for now. Only Tamara mattered.

Opening the door, he took the package and the purse into the house and then went back for Tamara.

Before he could get to her, she was trying to get up by herself. Quickly, he ran over to her.

"You know, I'm not that weak. It's just a twisted ankle," she said.

"You mean a sprained ankle."

Ignoring her effort to walk on her own, he lifted her into his arms like a baby and carried her inside. He knew what was probably going on in her head. She would probably think he was using every excuse to hold her close, to hold her in his arms. If she had the thought, she wasn't wrong.

When they entered the house, still carrying her in his arms, he asked, "What do you want..."

Reflexively, he looked at her. It was dark outside, so he hadn't really seen her well until now. When he looked at her, his breath caught for an instant. She was drenched, and she looked tired, but she was beautiful. Her wet hair was curly. The usually straightened hair had gone to its natural texture. And she looked so naturally beautiful.

Her brown eyes came quietly to his. The connection was so intense that it threatened to start up a fire of passion within him. He felt complete. He felt that she completed him, that she had always been a part of him, that her needs were his needs and his were hers.

In her eyes he saw something. Loneliness and pain. The look in her eyes made his heart want to explode with anger for causing her this much anguish.

He swallowed hard. "Take a shower first. Then we should take care of your ankle."

Very gently, he walked toward the bathroom.

"I can manage myself," she said.

Raymond ignored her statement and took her to the bathroom anyhow. "Don't put your weight on the leg that hurts and you should be fine for now. Get in the shower, I'll get your nighty."

"It's in the closets in..."

"I know where it is," he said gently. "I still remember."

She nodded her head. "Thanks."

****

Tamara finished taking her shower, put on her nightie and limped out of the bathroom. The warm air of the house surrounded her like an embrace. Raymond must have cranked up the heat.

Cautiously, she limped to the living room.

"You could have called for help," Raymond said as he walked over to her.

He was probably wondering if she was really as pitiful as she appeared, she thought. She couldn't bear for him to think that. She had humiliated herself enough for one day.

"Seriously, I can manage. I'm not that hurt."

He was a lot stronger than she was. She couldn't struggle with him. She let him put an arm around her again so she could lean on him as they walked.

He helped her to settle in the couch and then he crouched and held her ankle, about to start massaging it.

Palm over his hand, she said. "Don't."

He looked up at her. For a while he didn't say nothing. And then he began, his voice very calm, "When people need help, they run to you. You teach them to accept help without shame when they need it. Why don't you accept help when someone offers to help?"

She was staring at him, didn't take her eyes off him. She was at a loss on how to respond.

When she didn't reply, he began to rub her ankle. His hands were rough and strong, but he was gentle as he massaged her twisted ankle, and he didn't say a word.

He wasn't even looking at her.

His eyes were focused down on her delicate ankle.

For some reason—for no good reason— she felt like she might cry. Her eyes burn with hot tears and her throat tightened.

She'd always thought that he was a gentle and caring person. His loving and caring nature had melted her heart. She had been swept away by his charm.

Tamara still couldn't understand. How Raymond seemed to be so loving, so caring. How he had called her his heartbeat. How he could massage her ankle so gently even now.

And yet still have broken her heart one year ago.

She had to close her eyes to hold back her tears.

Raymond had moved on to place ice on her ankle. After which, he wrapped a bandage around it.

"Your ankle should feel better in the morning," he said.

She nodded. "Thanks. But really, I'll be fine. It's okay if you want to leave."

"I'll leave. But for now, you're stuck with my help. I'll leave when I see that you're okay."

The earlier he left the better for the both of them. The house was big, but it wouldn't be big enough for the both of them. There would be no way to get away from Raymond.

Whom she still wanted. No matter how deeply she knew she should never want him again. He was taken. Married. Meaning, he was unavailable.

She relaxed her back on the couch and pulled her leg out to inspect her ankle.

Raymond left and came back with Tylenol and a bottle of water. He surely knew his way around her house. She wasn't surprised. They made plenty memories in this house.

She took the pills. Then leaned back.

"Thanks."

She gave him a gentle look. "Your clothes are wet. You should take a warm shower and change into something else."

He had been nice to her. A little kindness in return for his kindness wouldn't hurt.

"I'll do that when I get back home. There's nothing to change into. Unless, of course, if you would lend me a skirt."

She smiled.

She tried to stand up from the couch. Raymond quickly rushed to her side.

She put up a hand to stop him. "I'll manage," she said. "But come with me."

They walked gently to the bedroom. In the bedroom, Tamara opened her wardrobe. And then she removed a white t-shirt and sweatpants from a hanger.

She handed it to him. "Unless you have outgrown them in a year."

Raymond took it from her, staring wide-eyed at Tamara, unable to hide his surprise. "You kept them all the while?"

She nodded, with a faint smile. "Yes. All of it. It made me feel as if you're around."

Raymond couldn't say anything. He kept looking at her. And Tamara noticed his eyes were watery. He was touched. And was trying not to cry.

"Go. Take a shower and change. I'll be in the living room."

Chapter 12

Raymond couldn't describe how he felt when Tamara said she couldn't trash his stuff. She kept them because it made her feel as if he was around. At that moment, his heart ached so much that he thought it might burst. More than anything he wanted to just hold her in his arms and cry that he was sorry. Sorry that he let himself be seduced by Dahlia. Sorry that he betrayed her. Sorry that he caused her so much pain.

But he doubted that Tamara would ever be able to forgive him. If only she would listen to him and let him explain how he got hooked in Dahlia's chains. But no matter how hard he tried to explain, Tamara was just not willing to listen.

The bathroom was overly familiar. He remembered every passionate sex they had in this damn shower. The memory haunted him too much.

His shower was quick.

He finished it and put on the white t-shirt over the sweatpants. When he walked back to the living room, he was most certain that he caught her staring at him. She had always loved it when he wore that. She'd called it simple, but sexy.

"I guess we should find something for dinner," Raymond said, walking into the kitchen.

Tamara stood up and followed him to the kitchen. "I'll help."

They both went together to investigate the refrigerator and it was close to empty.

"I haven't grocery shop in a while," Tamara said.

"Why should you? You never had the time to cook. And we can't order food on a day like this. The weather is really bad outside."

Tamara opened the freezer. "I think I still got some pancakes in here." Carefully, she brought out the pancakes from the freezer. "This should be ok, right?"

He nodded. "Yeah. We can microwave it and food is ready."

She handed the pancakes to Raymond and walked over to the cabinet. "I have honey too."

"Good."

She handed Raymond the honey, while Raymond continue to open all the cabinet, searching for plates. As he searched, he noticed the hinges of the cabinets were loosed. Without saying a word to Tamara, he walked to where he remembered the tools were kept and grabbed a screw driver. He got down on his knees and began to tighten the screw.

"What are you doing?" she demanded.

He didn't look at her. His eyes were fixed on

the cabinet. "What does it look like?"

"I don't know. You tell me."

"All the hinges are loose. I was just tightening them."

"Would you stop?" Tamara felt a deep resentment at the sight of Raymond working on the cabinet in her kitchen. "You don't need to do work around here. I'll fix it myself."

"Really? I'm sure the cabinet has been like this for quite a while. And you haven't fixed them yet."

"I already informed the maintenance service. They'll be here to fix it soon."

"Well, you don't have to pay to get little things done. I'm here. Use me."

"Yeah. You mean the same way you used me and dumped me for Dahlia?"

Her words felt like a punch. He felt the need to look her in the eye and correct what she had just said. But then he shrugged and ignored her. "I only have two more to go."

****

Tamara didn't mean to say that, but she did. And now she regretted it. It had been one year since the breakup. They had seen each other often in the last month and he had even tried to apologize for everything. She shouldn't be this bitter and angry anymore. But she just couldn't help it.

When Raymond finished fixing the cabinet, he walked over to where he had kept the package he helped brought in. "You finally bought kitchen stuff after I scolded you."

"You didn't scold me," she replied. "You were talking as if you knew everything about me. I bought the kitchen utensils just to prove you wrong."

"If I keep using that tactic, maybe I can get you to love cooking."

"I love cooking. I just don't have plenty time to spare."

He smiled. More like smiling to himself than to her. She wondered what was so amusing about her.

"Don't just stand there. Go to the living room. I'll bring dinner," he said, placing the pancakes into the microwave. He looked perfectly normal. He looked calm, matter of fact, he looked in control.

Tamara wished desperately that she was as controlled as he always was in face of awkwardness.

Oh! And he was damn hot in those sweatpants and t-shirt. He looked relaxed. And sexy. She couldn't resist watching as the muscles of his arm flexed when he worked on her cabinets. It reminded her of the movement of the muscles in his thigh when they....

Dirty thoughts...

Feeling the need to clear her mind, she walked over to the bar and poured herself a glass of red wine. "Do you want a beer?"

"Whatever you have there is fine."

She poured him wine too and took the glasses over to the table.

Few minutes later, Raymond brought the pancakes served with honey.

"How is your ankle?" he asked before taking a bite of his pancake.

"It's fine," she replied.

For the next few seconds, no one said anything. She felt strangely uncomfortable and she hated feeling that way. So she decided to avoid looking at him.

But then the silence was making things more awkward than she could bear. She decided she would start a conversation— one that would make him uncomfortable and make her feel better.

"It must have been hard," she said, her voice very modulated.

He looked at her. "What?"

She didn't shy away from his look. It made her feel in control. "Been married to Dahlia. It must have been hard when you found out about her affair with the gardener?"

"Dahlia finally told the truth?"

She shook her head. "No. But I'm good at what I do. Connecting the dots seems to be one of my super ability." *Except I couldn't connect the dots and know that you will leave me for Dahlia.* She said in her mind.

"Yes," he said. "It was hard." His brown eyes now focused on her for real, not looking past her the way he'd been doing since they started eating. "It was a slur on my manhood. I felt as if I wasn't man enough. I felt rejected. It was hard."

She thought knowing that it was hard for him

would make her feel good. But, obviously, she was wrong. Her heart went out to him. He had had a hard life. She knew what his life had been like. She knew how the fact that his father rejected him from birth had crushed him. Now, when he said he felt rejected, she understood him perfectly.

"If you had told me what she did, I would have been on your side. Why were you covering up for her?"

He took a slow sip of wine, mostly to pause. "Because I didn't want to drag her dignity through the mud and..."

"What?" she interrupted, sounding sharper than she had intended. "She lost her dignity when she decided to screw her gardener, a 17 year old boy."

Realizing that she had yelled unnecessarily, she tried to calm herself. "There are not many men who would be concern about her dignity like you did. You're a very good person, Raymond Brock."

His eyes came boldly to hers again. "You're a good person too, Tamara Price. You're a very strong woman, the strongest I've ever known." He gave her a smile. It was a beautiful, tempting smile. It made her want to just lean closer and kiss those succulent lips.

She'd held his gaze for too long. She withdrew her gaze and smiled in turn.

They finished the rest of their meal in silence. When they'd washed up, she relaxed on the couch, turned on the TV and tuned to CNN.

"Anything going on?" he asked, sitting beside her on the couch.

She shook her head. "Nothing. Just news on the weather."

For the next few minutes, they were awkwardly quiet. Their body took notice of each other and the atmosphere was tensed. They would look at each other once in a while and their eyes met. Tamara would look away quickly, but Raymond wouldn't take his eyes off her.

Tamara was uncomfortable, and she hated feeling that way. "I'll use the bathroom."

Anything to escape the awkwardness. Anything to prevent her from grabbing him and making passionate love to him on that couch.

She got up to go to the bathroom. When she got there, she started flapping her hands frantically like she does when she was unnerved. She told herself to relax, closed her eyes breathing in and out.

Staring at her reflection in the mirror, she was smoothing down her hair when she realized what she was doing.

Making sure she looked pretty for when she saw Raymond again.

Angry at herself, she decided to roughen up her hair a little back to the way it was. She didn't forget to flush the toilet to make it look like she actually did use it.

She was walking back to the living room when she stepped on her ankle wrong. She went down, hurting her ankle more in the process.

She bit her lip in pain.

She was trying to struggle to get up when Raymond appeared in front of her. He was the last person she wanted to see. He had recently just told her that she was the strongest woman he had ever known. Now, she was showing the direct opposite of strength.

Raymond moved very quickly to pull her up. "What happened?"

"Nothing," she said, clearly embarrassed. "I fell, but I'm fine."

He put an arm around her for support. "Why didn't you call for help?"

"Because I don't need help."

Raymond ignored her comment and helped her back to the couch. When Raymond sat beside her on the couch, things went back to the way it was. Tense.

She tried to concentrate on the TV, her heart pounding heavily, thinking he was going to grab her any minute.

Again, she decided to start a conversation. "Dahlia knows the big secret."

"I know." He wasn't surprised at all.

"You told her?"

He shook his head. "No, I didn't. But I know she knows."

She took a quick look at him. "Then you know her game plan. She has her eyes on the whole Connor wealth."

"I thought so."

"Do you know she might hurt you, I mean kill you, if necessary?"

"I don't think she is capable."

"I think she's desperate," she said. "My advice to you, get your divorce done as quickly as possible. If you can't, you should be very careful. Hire a body guard. If she's your next of kin, change it immediately. Prepare a will, just in case. My team and I would start to investigate her from tomorrow. I want to know who told her the big secret. So I'm going to invite the 15 people who knew that you are a Connor. One of them must have leaked the secret."

"Mara," he said, trying to make his voice gentle but firm. "This issue is very big, bigger than what you think. Please, don't try to fix it for me. Don't get involved with it. I'll never forgive myself if any danger comes to you. Please, let me fix it. Don't get involved."

"Too late. I'm involved already."

"Mara!" he growled in a very sexy voice.

"Okay," she replied. "I won't get involved."

"I know you too much to believe that you won't actually involve yourself."

She gave a slight smile.

"Tell me, Mara. You love helping people, but you won't let anyone help you. Why?"

She swallowed the lumps that rose in her throat, aware that the conversation had taken a subtle shift. For one long second, Tamara didn't respond. She looked at him. His eyes met the gaze of her brown eyes. "Because you help me with everything. You always do everything for me. You take out the trash, fix things in the house, do the grocery and when you left, for a long time, I was helpless, pitiful and pathetic. It took me quite a while to start doing things myself, but once I started, I learned that people aren't exactly doing you a favor when they help you all the time."

"Mara."

"It's late," she interrupted. "I'll go to bed now."

"Okay."

He put an arm around her and led her to bed. Then he went back to grab some ice. He placed it on her ankle and then put the bandage on again.

Very gently, he helped her relax on the bed and then covered her with a blanket. Crouching beside the bed, he said, "Sleep well. I see that you are fine. So I'll leave now."

Releasing her hand from inside the blanket, she held Raymond's hand. "The weather is still bad outside. Driving in this kind of weather and this late is dangerous..."

"Don't worry too much about me. I'll be fine."

She released his hold on him and then he covered her again with the blanket. "Good night, Mara," he said and walked out of the room.

Chapter 13

Really?

Goodnight?

That's all the man could say or do?

She'd told him to stay. She'd been more than ready to sleep with him. She wanted him. Like she had not wanted anyone in the last one year. She loved him. Respected him. Melted into his arms every time he carried her like a baby, trying to support her movements.

And he'd left. And said only a measly goodnight.

Maybe he hadn't wanted her. If he had, he wouldn't just leave.

Such a fool she'd been. Thinking that Raymond wanted her as much as she did. But if he hadn't wanted her, why the hell was he giving the wrong signals? Meeting her gaze, holding her close in the pretense that he was helping, fixing things around the house like a man who was doing every good deed to get laid.

The man was an idiot...

She rolled over to her side, keeping her thighs

tightly closed together. She was going to force herself to sleep when she heard the door opened.

She sat up.

Her eyes fell on Raymond.

"What?" she asked.

He walked over to her side and sat opposite her on the bed, staring into her eyes. The stare was different. More intense.

"Mara," he called with a deep sexy voice.

She felt emotions rushed through her and her whole body trembled at the vibrations his deep voice had caused. Her skin heated. Her breathing became shallow.

Just once, she told herself as she decided that she needed no more encouragement. She'd go after what she wanted. Him.

Just this once, she'd do this.

And never again.

But she'd to have it this one time, or she'd go mad.

She wanted to lean closer and kiss him when he drew her head closer toward his until their lips met. It wasn't demanding or controlling—just gentle and almost needy.

Fames of uncontrolled need licked through her and she couldn't help but respond. She lowered her back in pleasure, opening her mouth to feel him more deeply as he lay on top of her. "I almost thought you won't make a move."

He tilted his head to deepen the kiss. "I didn't know if you want me to."

Their kiss was just as intense and hungry as the other night they had dinner, but he seemed different somehow. He seemed more connected to her and less of pure lust. Or maybe that was just her imagination.

"Mara," he said huskily, when he pulled away but just to press soft little kisses on the corner of her mouth. "Your ankle. Is it okay…"

She nodded and laughed softly.

"Good," he said thickly and leaned down into another kiss.

When his hand reached for her nightie, she was already tugging it off. Her hands were still tangled in the dress above her head when he bent down, suckled one nipple in his wet mouth and covered the other with his palm.

"Damn! I miss those. They're beautiful," he said under his breath.

She smiled, flexed her back and leaned toward him, offering him more.

Feeling and sensation swelled up inside of her and she raised her hips to press against his hard body. When his mouth moved over her breasts, smooching and kissing her and teasing her, she knew what it was like to feel want, need and desire simultaneously stroking her into a heated passion.

"Mara," he murmured, kissing his way down her body, caressing her body with his hot, velvety tongue. "Mara, tell me you don't want to do this, and I'll stop."

She wanted him badly. She knew it was foolish. And wrong. And it would make everything so much harder.

But none of that mattered in the moment.

"I want to do this," she moaned through ragged breath.

Hands free at last, she tugged at his shirt, pulling it over his head and flipping it on the ground next to them.

A soft moan of pleasure escaped through her lips as his magnificent bare chest touched hers. Her supersensitive nipples hardened under his chest as they rubbed each other, while their kisses became more intense.

He eased his way down with more hot, wet kisses on her stomach.

"I want to taste you."

Tamara's body quivered with delicious anticipation.

With his hands, he gently spread her thigh and placed his mouth over the most sensitive part of her body. His tongue hurried along the edge, teasing her.

She grabbed his head, caressed his neatly cut hair and pushed his head against her, breathing his name and pleading to stop the teasing and taste her.

She could feel his smile as he worked her panties down, revealing her perfectly moist opening to him.

He whispered her name very softly, then gently stroke her with his tongue. Heat and moisture and pleasure fused between her leg and at that moment, she knew what it was to live a fantasy. Placing her hand on his head, she lifted her hip greedily for more.

Then his mouth moved around the front,

using his slow, wet, torturous tongue between her leg, darting it around the most sensitive part, and then sucking her harder and deeper and faster until she gasped and exploded in his mouth.

Before she'd recovered, he was kissing his way back up, breathing her name and holding her tight.

Her hands with a deep need went down to his sweatpants. "Let me, Raymond."

"Ray." He brushed his mouth against her cheeks, and then placed a sensual kiss upon her lips. "You used to call me Ray."

Slowly, Tamara lowered his sweatpants and then softly took him. Pleasure gnawed at him the moment Tamara's fingers closed over his flesh. He groaned softly in her ear as she slid along the length of his erection, caressing him, stroking him so softly, so gently a grunt of desire caught in his throat.

The wanton need to enter into her had the whole of his body throbbing and shaking.

"Mara," he whispered. "You're going to kill me."

She smiled and eased herself above him, their gazes locked on each other as she straddled him, gorgeous and naked with her long, curly hair tumbling over her shoulders and tickling her breasts. He murmured her name, hypnotized by the sight of her black, hardened nipple. She leaned closer, her bare breast rubbing against his.

With one quick movement he rolled over on the bed, positioning himself on top of her. His erection sank completely into her soft wet hole, causing him to suck in a breath.

He lifted her hip and thrust into her, his hips rocking back and forth.

With each needy thrust into her, their rhythm increased, their labored breath became more ragged. Wanting to be connected to her at every point till the end, he lowered himself and placed the smallest of kisses on her lips, gazing deep into her eyes, loving the way she looked back at him with her expression drowsy with passion.

She clutched him tighter, feeling his muscles beneath her fingers as they dug into the flesh of his shoulders. She pulled him into her with her heels, forcing him deeper inside her, deeper than she thought she could bear, but wanting him so much that she thought he would somehow become part of her.

Finally the raging storm of the intense pleasure became unbearable, squeezing his heart until he finally gave in, kissing her and breathing her name until he emptied everything inside Mara...and then he collapsed on top of her, his face buried in the hollow of her shoulder as she softly kissed the side of his head.

Chapter 14

The first ray of dawn had just stretched out into the room when Tamara Price woke up. Her ankle still ached a little, her lady part was tender and her head pounded. She looked over beside her and saw that Raymond's side of the bed was empty.

He was gone.

Again.

With a sharp pain in her chest, she sat up and called, "Ray! Ray!" Waiting for an answer she knew wasn't coming, she glanced around…and then she saw a small note on Raymond's side of the bed.

She had always known Raymond to be the love-letter type. Quickly, she grabbed the letter.

Baby,

You slept like a baby, didn't want to wake you up. I had to leave early cos I had some business to attend to. I'll see you at lunch.

Oh! Place an ice on your ankle if it still hurts, or else...you won't be able to put on those Chrysler Building heels today.

Kisses,
Ray.

She smiled. The man still cared about her and her heels. She remembered how— in the past— he always said her heels were as high as the Chrysler building. She read the note four more times and she smiled every time she read the heels part.

She was going to read for the fifth time when reality set in for her. Raymond wasn't bothered by what happened between them. He had moved on as if everything had gone back to the way it used to be between them, as if they had gone back to being a couple.

Last night was full of intense pleasure, she wouldn't deny that, but the guilt she felt right now was as full and intense as the pleasure she had felt the night before.

What had she done? What was she thinking?

She was supposed to be fixing his marriage with Dahlia and she slept with him, instead, ruining the marriage even more.

The thought that she had slept with a married man caused an irritation in her stomach and she felt like she could throw up. Quickly, she threw the note in the drawer and ran to the bathroom.

She opened her mouth, nothing spewed out from it. Tears filled her eyes, but she didn't shed them.

She didn't start to cry until she stepped under the shower.

As she scrubbed Raymond off her body, she sobbed as quietly as she could. A night full of intimacy, passion and pleasure followed by a guilt-filled morning.

By the time she finished taking her shower, she had gotten herself under control. She was sitting in front of the mirror trying to flat iron her hair when it hit her that she was no different from Dahlia. Whatever evil Dahlia had done to her had been nullified the moment she slept with Raymond. She was no different from Dahlia and that hurt her even more.

Dropping the flat iron, she went back to bed. She decided she would stay in bed throughout today. She wouldn't go nowhere. How would she dare to show her adulterous face to the world? She was supposed to stand for good morals. She was the face of hope in a dying marriage. And now she had become the death that would destroy Raymond's marriage.

Pain knotted her heart and she pulled the cover over her head. Swallowing, she fought back the tears that seemed to come so easily.

She didn't know how long she stayed in bed, but for each passing minute, the pain in her heart deepened.

She was deep in thought when she heard the door opened. Slowly, she sat up to see who it was.

It was Drake.

He stood at the door for some seconds, staring

at her. "What's the problem, Tamara?"

She must really look pathetic right now, but that didn't matter. Drake had seen her in worst moment.

When she didn't respond, he walked gently over and sat beside her on the bed. He didn't sit very close— just close.

"When I waited for two hours and didn't see you at work, I knew you probably couldn't get out of bed." He looked at her. "I'm not going to ask you what the problem is." He shook his head. "No, no, but you don't get to stay in bed and sleep your problem away. Sometimes, shit happens, but you have to pull it together, suck it up and rush into battle. And on the battle field, you might get hurt. But you don't get to stop and cry over the pain. You move on, hang in there, and persevere until the end. Until the end! That was your rule! Your standard! You are Tamara Price. You have responsibilities! People, couples, depend on you. Oh! You think you can only be that person as long as you don't have any problems, as long as you don't have any flaws, as long as you are perfect. No, Tamara. You better get your ass together and go back to being who you are!"

He stood up speedily from the bed and walked toward the door. When he got to the door, he stopped and turned to look at her. "Bishop Shepherd hit his wife again today, until she was at the brink of death. She has refused to go ahead with the divorce plan; you might want to start the day's work by visiting her at the City hospital. And I found out that Bishop Shepherd has anger management problem since he was a teenager. He enrolled himself in anger management class way before he became a preacher, but he dropped out after one or two sessions. The interesting part is, Linda knows about his anger management problem. " He walked out and shut the door.

It was as if Drake's words were exactly what she needed to get out of bed. Quickly, she hurried to put on her clothes, get her makeup done and rushed out of the house.

Chapter 15

When Tamara walked in to the ward, she couldn't believe her eyes. Linda shepherd's body was covered with bruises— bruises that were caused by her husband. Women could be pathetic sometimes, she said to herself. How could this woman still choose to want to be with a man that kept hitting her over and over again? She wouldn't even agree to go ahead with the fake divorce plans. Did she love her husband so much that he would let him beat her to death or was she just being an idiot?

You're not very different from Linda, she told herself. Raymond had hurt her—maybe not physically, but emotionally. Yet, she still ran into his arms last night.

"It's not as bad as it looks. Doctor said I can go home today," Linda said with a faint smile.

Tamara didn't respond.

"I told the doctor that I fell," Linda said with teary eyes. "I couldn't tell him the truth. That my husband beat me. I just said that I fell." She paused for a while before she continued. "I can't go ahead with the divorce plan. Please, Tamara, find another way to help me."

Tamara swallowed hard. She was breathing heavily from the weight of the words she was about to say. "Before, when I said it's not your fault, I was wrong. It is your fault."

Linda stared wide-eyed.

Tamara nodded her head. "Yes. It's your fault. It is NOT your fault that he beats you, but it is your fault for letting him get away it and letting him keep beating you again and again."

Tears ran down Linda's cheek. "Tamara, stop!"

"You love him. I know you do, but that doesn't mean you have to keep covering up for him. He keeps beating you because you let him. You're the reason he has so many flaws. You're the reason he's not trying to make himself better. You give him everything he asks for, you cover up for him, you clean up his mess and that is not how to love someone. You're destroying him and destroying yourself too. It's not your fault that he beats you, but protecting his reputation by covering up for him and not talking him into taking those anger management classes again, that is your fault."

Linda was sobbing quietly.

Tamara relaxed, satisfied at having made her point and knowing that her words had gotten to her. She walked speedily out of the ward, placing a call to Drake as she did.

"Drake?"

"Yes, Tamara," Drake replied.

"Get me an address for Bishop Shepherd.

Linda is going to go ahead with the divorce plans and I need to get to the preacher first."

"Linda told you she'd go ahead with the divorce?"

"No, she didn't."

"So how do you know she's going to go ahead with the plan?"

"I just know. Are you going to give me the address?" Tamara asked.

"I'll text you."

"Already," she said and hung up.

****

Tamara walked into the lobby of the Preacher's office. "Please, I'd like to see Bishop Shepherd."

"The Bishop is not counseling today. Do you have an appointment with him?"

Before she could respond, Tamara heard her phone rang. She gestured to the receptionist to give her a second while she checked to see who it was. Raymond. Ignoring the call, she looked back at the receptionist. "No, I don't have an appointment. Tell him it's Tamara Price. I'm representing his wife and it's urgent that I speak to him."

"Tamara Price?"

She nodded.

"Really?" She put up a bright smile. "I'm so glad to finally meet you. My sister wouldn't stop talking about how you help save her marriage." She stood from her seat and reached to give

Tamara a quick hug.

Tamara returned her hug with a bright smile.

"I'll tell the Bishop that you're here."

She picked up her desk phone and informed the Bishop about her. "He said to let you come in."

"Thanks," Tamara said and began to walk into the Bishop's office.

"Wait," the receptionist said. "If you are representing the Bishop's wife, it means they're having problems with their marriage."

Tamara gave a sarcastic smile. "If the story leaks out, you won't be smiling at me the next time we see," she said. "Understand?"

"I won't tell anyone."

"Good."

Tamara opened the door and walked into the Bishop's office. "Good afternoon, Bishop."

"Afternoon, Miss Price," the Bishop said. "Please have a seat."

Tamara sat in the arm chair opposite of him, dropping her purse on the floor.

"I've heard quite a lot about you. I'm happy to finally meet you. You save people's marriages. The bible says God hates divorce. By helping people to save their marriages, you're one of the few who is doing God's work without even knowing it."

Tamara smiled. "Thank you."

"God will continue to bless you and give you strength."

"Amen."

Placing his hands on the table, he leaned

forward. "How can I help you, Miss Price?"

Tamara relaxed her back on the arm chair. "I'm here on behalf of your wife. Your wife would be filing for divorce and..."

He cut her off. "What?"

Tamara continued in the same pace. "Your wife would be filing for divorce and..."

"You're joking, right?"

"Your wife would be filing for divorce and I'm here to let you know that she wants the divorce to be amicable as humanly possible."

"My wife has no reason to file for divorce."

Modulating her voice as if she was saying something nice, she continued. "If you agree to an amicable divorce, my client has agreed to cite the reason for divorce as irreconcilable differences. But if you disagree, the reason will be domestic violence, followed by charges of wife battery."

His palm became a fist and hit the table. "This is outrageous! I did not beat my wife."

"Then what is your wife doing at the City hospital right now?"

"She fell from the stairs and I took her to the hospital."

Tamara shot him a glare. "That's not true." Her voice was beginning to lose the gentle touch. "That's the lie you told at the hospital to cover up your sins. By the way, Bishop, if you truly understood the bible, you would know that lying and trying to cover up your sins is a sin before God."

He rose fiercely from his chair. "Stop! Stop now!"

"Or what? You're going to beat me the same way you've been beating your wife for the past ten years?"

"I did not beat my wife!" he barked.

Standing up to meet his height, she lifted her phone to his face. "Right here, I have pictures of the bruises you gave to your wife. Your wife is at the hospital ready to tell the world what you've done to her in the last ten years. The only reason she is not talking yet is because I told her not to. I told her I will negotiate with you a peaceful divorce and agree to give the custody of the kids to your wife."

He locked eye with her, frowning. "My wife loves me. She won't leave me."

"Don't be so sure."

Tamara bent down to pick her purse and turned to leave.

"Miss Price, you are not in support of divorce. You save marriages! That's what you do."

"Bishop, till today I have helped save more than 50 marriages and helped dissolved more than ten marriages. So I dare say I can decide to do any at a particular time. I'm very good at both. And for your case, I'm choosing to help dissolve this marriage because a wife beater like you doesn't deserve a family."

"You think you have the right to play God?" he yelled. "You think you have some power to decide the marriage that is worth saving and the one that's not. God joined the couples together and He alone has the power to separate them."

She nodded her head and then turned to

leave. "Well, Bishop, let's just assume that God is doing that through me and the law."

"Your mother," he said. "I heard she is training to become a pastor. I'm sure she thought you that the bible says God hates divorce."

She turned to face him. "You know quite a lot about me. But you didn't do your homework right, because if you did, you will know that my mother also has three divorces on her name. And one of her husbands was a wife beater like you."

"Miss Price!"

She walked closer to him, face closed. "Let me make it clear, Bishop. This is a fair warning. My client will give you the petition for dissolution of marriage and all you have to do is sign them without questions or problems. You will also agree to let your wife take the custody of the kids. Also, since the divorce proceeding is starting today, you have up to 24 hours to move out of your marital home or else... I will let the press know about how you've been beating your wife. I'll make your wife press domestic battery charges against you. I'll take you to court and I'll win. I always do. And then it will make a very interesting headline: famous preacher, Bishop Shepherd, jailed for battery. Your image would be tarnished and the reputation you love so much will be destroyed. So, whatever way you choose to play this game, you lose! Play the game my way, agree to my terms and we will have a quiet divorce and your reputation might still be saved." She withdrew her gaze and began to walk away. "Good day, Bishop!"

As she walked out of the Bishop's office, her phone rang.

It was Raymond.

She picked the call. "What?" she said, almost yelling.

"Hi, Mara, you've been ignoring my calls,"

"Stop calling my phone!"

"Mara, what...You...I thought...I thought we were okay."

At that moment, she had walked to the parking lot. Opening the car door, she said, "You thought wrong, Ray. You didn't expect last night to mean something, do you? 'Cause it meant nothing."

She hung up and entered the car. Her heart ached in pain and tears gathered in her eyes. She lied. Last night had meant something to her. Last night meant a lot to her. After a few seconds, she wiped her tears and pulled onto the street.

When Tamara got home, she showered and made some sandwiches, but she was still restless as night tightened around the house. Things got worse when she heard her doorbell rang. She ran to the door to check.

It was Raymond.

She leaned on the door, each sound of the doorbell breaking her heart all over again. Her phone rang and it was Raymond. Instead of opening the door or picking his call, she sat back down at the door and cried.

Few minutes later, the doorbell stopped ringing.

Raymond left.

Quietly, Tamara went to bed. Before she slept, she opened her drawer, picked the note Raymond had left that morning and read again.

Baby,

You slept like a baby, didn't want to wake you up. I had to leave early cos I had some business to attend to. I'll see you at lunch.

Oh! Place an ice on your ankle if it still hurts, or else...you won't be able to put on those Chrysler Building heels today.

Kisses,
Ray.

Tears trickled down her cheeks, but it was alright. Everything was alright. She was paying for her mistakes. Everyone makes mistake and everyone pays a price. She had been the one who was stupid to have jumped into bed with him, so she now had to pay the price.

She loved Raymond, but she wouldn't continue the affair. She wanted to be more than a mistress to him. She wanted to be his one and only choice. Not a second choice after a failed marriage.

She would protect him, fight his battles and love him from afar. She could only hope that, one day, his hands would wipe away the tears that he caused her to shed.

Chapter 16

Raymond had no idea what the hell he was thinking. In fact, he wasn't thinking at all. The woman had ignited the fire of passion that was once sprouted between them. She had awakened a hunger that refused to be ignored. And he had given in to the temptation.

That night. It meant a lot to him. But Mara. Mara said it meant nothing. He didn't believe her, though. What happened between them wasn't just physical. No matter what Mara thought, he knew there was something real between them. There had always been something real between them. He knew he blew it about a year ago, but even Mara didn't know the whole story with it. He never wanted to end what they had. Even when he was married to Dahlia, he never stopped loving Mara. His heart, the whole of him was owned by Mara. He never wanted to not be with her. What they had then was real and what they had now was real too. He wasn't going to just give up on it, because Mara was trying to run away from it.

A slight knock on the door broke through his reverie. "Come in," he said.

Anita walked in. "Hello,"

"Hi, Anita. How's your day been?"

"Good." She opened a folder and placed it on the table before him. "Please, sign here."

Raymond read through very quickly, signed the document and handed it back to Anita.

"Do you need me to help prepare for your trip tomorrow?"

Raymond raised a brow. "What trip?"

"Your trip to Rhode Island. Your flight is 9.a.m tomorrow morning."

"Oh! I totally forgot about that. Go ahead and reschedule the trip for next week or two weeks from now."

Anita stared wide-eyed. "You're joking, right?"

"Yes. Reschedule."

"This would be the third time I'm rescheduling this same trip."

Raymond nodded. "Okay. Reschedule again."

In exasperation, she hit her forehead with her palm and turned to leave.

"Anita!" Raymond called.

She halted. "Yes."

"Please, have a seat." He pointed to the arm chair opposite of him. "I'd like to have a word with you."

She sat opposite of him. "Is this business or personal?"

Raymond pulled his brow together in a mischievous frown. "You're my personal assistant. Not business assistant. So, yes, this is personal."

Anita didn't respond.

Raymond relaxed his back on the chair, and looking at Anita, he asked, "Why do women always say one thing but mean another?"

"Excuse me?"

"Yeah, you heard me. Most women lie about their feelings. And because you're a woman, I thought you would be able to tell me why."

Anita stood up from the chair and started to leave. "Have a nice day."

Raymond scowled. "Anita, you're dangerously treading close to losing your job."

Anita smiled. "You mean the job where I make travel plans and schedule meetings that you don't honor."

"Anita..." Raymond warned.

"Alright, if I must answer. If a woman doesn't talk true of her feelings, the man should accept it and SUFFER IN SILENCE." She emphasized the "suffer in silence".

"Suffer in silence? That's my word. Anita, you're throwing my words back in my face."

Anita giggled.

"You're fired!" Raymond said.

"Bye. See you tomorrow."

With no malice in his voice, Raymond replied, "Yeah. See you tomorrow. My regards to your husband."

****

"From this moment, Raymond Brock has

become our client whether he knows it or not." Tamara announced as everyone settled in the conference room, listening intently to her, her brown eyes concentrating on everyone.

"Does that mean we are finally giving up on trying to save an already broken marriage?" Sherry asked.

Tamara shook her head in disagreement. "It means we are protecting Raymond Brock." Tamara stood up and folded her arms. "Dahlia has issued a threat to kill Raymond and I think she is desperate enough to actually do it." She started to pace back and forth. "Right now, we are working on the assumption that Dahlia wants to kill Raymond in order to get her hands on the Connor wealth. We can't go to the police yet because my assumptions aren't enough evidence. So, we have to think of how we can protect Raymond from Dahlia." She glanced at them. "Ideas! I need ideas!"

"I think we should start from the point where Dahlia accused you of having an affair with Raymond. Is that true?" Sherry asked.

Tamara scowled. "Whether I'm having an affair with Raymond or not is not any of your damn business." The scowl on her beautiful face deepened. "I need ideas!"

"Well," Megan began. "You said it was supposed to be a secret that Raymond is a Connor."

Tamara nodded in agreement. "Yeah. Only 15 of us knew. Since you guys now knows, that makes it 18 of us."

"Definitely, someone must have told Dahlia," Megan replied. "And if someone told her, it's best to assume that Dahlia isn't working alone. When it comes to family wealth, there's always a conspiracy. So we might have more problems on our hands than we know."

Sherry cleared her throat. "Please, I have a quick question."

All attention shifted to her.

She shivered and blinked hard. "Aren't we divorce attorneys? Why are we suddenly doing the work of a detective?"

Tamara studied Sherry and noticed the fear in her eyes. "Because someone I care about is about to get hurt and I have to save him," Tamara replied. "This is probably too much for you. It's okay if you don't want to be part of it."

"Really?" Sherry asked.

"Yes, really."

"Thank you."

Sherry picked up her folder and walked out of the conference room.

Tamara shifted her gaze back to Megan and Drake. "More ideas."

Drake cleared his throat. "I believe Dahlia wants to stay married to Raymond in order for her to get the chance to kill Raymond. Even if there's a conspiracy somewhere and Dahlia is not working alone, there's a possibility that she is the only one close enough to actually finish off Raymond."

Tamara sat back down on the chair. Elbows on the table and heads down, she was lost in thought for a while. After few seconds, she lifted her head. "I agree with you, Drake. If Dahlia is asking for more time to stay married to Raymond, she's probably waiting for the best chance to finish him." She looked at Drake. "Drake," she called. Before she could say anything, the door opened.

Tamara looked toward the door.

"Sherry?"

"Bishop Shepherd is here. He is asking to see you."

Tamara ignored her and turned to Drake. "Drake, please find a way to search Dahlia's house for any kind of weapon. Pay close attention to chemicals most especially Arsenic, mercury and selenium."

Drake arched a brow. "You think she might be planning to slowly poison him over a period of time?"

Tamara nodded. "I think she already started. That explains why she would ask for more time?"

"Can I say something, please? Sherry asked.

Tamara signaled her to go ahead.

"I was just wondering how Drake is going to search Dahlia's home. He can't go to the police, no search warrant and I know Drake isn't going to go to Dahlia to ask nicely."

Drake found a polite smile. "Don't worry, Sherry. I'm not going to break in."

Tamara shifted her gaze to Megan. "Megan, I'm going to give you the names of people who knew about Raymond being a Connor. I need you to invite them all to a meeting."

Megan nodded. "Okay."

Tamara glanced at her watch and then back at Sherry. "Tell Bishop Shepherd to please come in."

Chapter 17

Bishop Shepherd came in and took the seat next to Tamara.

Tamara's eyes searched his face keenly. As if she was looking for something. Perhaps a shade of soberness. She was right. His eyes were red like someone who had been crying. So men do cry, Tamara said to herself.

"Miss Price, you have to help me." His voice was desperate.

"You're not my client," she replied. "I can't help you."

"I know we started off on the wrong foot, and I'm sorry," he said impatiently. "But please, help me. I've heard all about you. You try your best to save marriages. Please help me. I don't want to lose my wife."

Tamara steepled her fingers under her chin, elbows on the armrests of her chair. But said nothing.

"My wife gave me this," he said hurriedly as he handed a document to Tamara.

Tamara took the document and read through

in a split second. "This is the petition for dissolution of marriage. All you have to do is sign it.

Close to tears, he said, "Tamara, I can't. I can't sign this. I don't want to lose Linda. I don't want to lose my wife."

Tamara gave the document back to him. "I think you should be telling this to her, not to me."

"I did. I begged her, pleaded with her, but she wouldn't change her mind." He paused for a second to swallow. "It was as if she was determined to leave. I never knew Linda was capable of this."

She straightened her face. "You never knew she was capable of asking for a divorce?" Tamara asked. "Is that why you've been beating her all these years?"

He let out a deep breath, letting it out slowly. "I'm sorry. I'm very sorry for everything." He looked deeply into Tamara's eyes. "Please, help me plead with my wife. I'll be a better person for her. I'll control my anger. I'll get help. I'll take the anger management class."

Tamara held his gaze and studied him. "Are you saying that you're ready to put your reputation on the line and get help?"

He nodded his head slowly.

Tamara put her hands on the table and leaned closer. "The headlines. It's going to say: Famous Preacher, Bishop Shepherd, who preached against anger for years actually has anger problem, now takes anger management class. It's going to get pretty ugly."

"It doesn't matter. I can give it all for Linda. She deserves it." His eyes told that he meant it.

Tamara's voice turned gentler. "Did you tell this to Linda? Did you tell her that you're ready to get help?"

"Yes, I did," the bishop said. "But Linda refused to accept me still."

Tamara lowered her head in thought for a moment. When she looked back up, she glanced at Megan who was also present in the conference room. "Megan, please, search for the best anger management class. Go ahead and enroll him into class when you find one and schedule him for a one on one session with a therapist."

Looking back at the bishop, she said, "I'll talk to your wife only on one condition."

He looked at Tamara, paying attention. "Anything."

Tamara nodded. "Okay," she said. "I understand that you are ready to get help. But it's most likely that you may relapse again. If and when you relapse, if you as much as yell at your wife let alone beat her, ever again, the deal is off the table. I'm going to get your wife out of the marriage. And your kids."

"I won't relapse. I'll try. God will help me."

"Pray well, Bishop."

He didn't respond.

"Alright. I'll talk to your wife. You can go for now."

He managed a smile. "Thanks."

Immediately Bishop Shepherd walked out of the room, Tamara took her cell phone and placed a call to Linda.

"Hello, Tamara," Linda said. "I asked him for divorce. I made my acting so real that he was going crazy, thinking I'm actually capable of it." She kept talking on and on about how she actually was bold enough to stand up to her husband. "I did well, didn't I?"

Tamara smiled. "Yes. You did good. Your husband was here. He was filled with remorse. He promised to get help, take anger management classes and even talk to a therapist if necessary."

"WOW!" She sounded so excited. "That's good news, right?"

"I don't know, Linda," Tamara said. "He might agree to get help for now. What if he relapses and he goes back to being who he is. Are you sure you want to take the risk and stay married to him?"

For a few seconds, Linda didn't respond.

"Linda!" Tamara called. "Are you there?"

"He beats me," Linda began gently, her voice shaky. "But when he is calm and the anger is gone, he goes on his knees, tears in his eyes; he'd cried that he was sorry. And I'll ask him to get help, but he wouldn't agree to it. He was afraid of ruining his reputation." She was quiet for another long second. "If now, he is putting his reputation on the line to get help, isn't it a good thing that he is trying to be better? His sacrifice should worth something. As a good wife, I should stick with him and help him get better. Tamara, you won't understand how much I've wanted him to at least try to get better. I wanted to see him trying. And I am so very happy that he is now trying to be better for me. It is good news, Tamara. Thank you very much for your help."

"You're always welcome, Linda. And I wish you a happy married life."

"Thank you."

When Tamara got home, as she lay on her bed to sleep, Linda's words kept repeating itself in her head. *As a good wife, I should stick with him and help him get better. Tamara, you won't understand how much I've wanted him to at least try to get better. I wanted to see him trying.*

Raymond was trying to be better, trying to make up for all the pain he'd caused her, but she kept pushing him away. Shouldn't she be sticking with her man like Linda, especially when his life could be in danger?

The thought that his life could be in danger hit her again. She felt the need to warn him. Quickly, she took her cell phone and placed a call to Raymond. He picked the call almost immediately.

"Mara," he said and let out a deep breath.

The way he called her name with all that emotions made her missed him even more. She hugged her pillow tightly, wishing he could be there with her, wishing she could bring herself to tell him that she missed him, loved him and that more than anything, she wanted him. But she couldn't.

"Mara," he said again. "Are you there?"

She didn't respond.

Silence roared in his ears.

Thousands of emotions rushed through her

and she felt a lump in her throat. She didn't want Raymond to hear her cry. Quietly, she hung up the phone.

And then she texted him. *Hello Ray, please, don't eat at home. Eat out for the meantime. Be safe.*

Few seconds later, her phone was ringing again. She checked to see who it was.

Raymond.

Ignoring the call, she held her pillow tightly. Tears filled her eyes and she couldn't tell how long she cried before she finally fell asleep.

Chapter 18

When the fifteen was settled in their chair, Tamara walked in confidently to the conference room with her army of lawyers— Drake, Megan and Sherry.

Her eyes scanned the room, making sure they were all in attendant. The fifteen mainly consist of shareholders at Connor Corp, the directors, domestic staff of the Connor and the two Connor brothers.

"Sorry to keep you waiting," she said.

Before she could say further, some of them began to talk. It started from a murmur and then it blew up into chaos, shouting on top of their voices, arguing with each other trying to make a point, trying to ask why Tamara brought them back into this when they've all moved on.

"Calm down," Drake pleaded.

When they didn't listen, Megan yelled, "Stop!"

The chaos blew up when some of them began to pick a fight with each other. The room heated up! Noise increased. When Tamara couldn't take it any longer, her palm became a fist and hit the table.

"Quiet!" she yelled.

The room went dead silent in a second. But then the silence was disturbed when Tamara began to cough. The yell had caused a mild dryness in her throat and she coughed. They rushed to give her a bottle of water which was on the table for each of them.

Dammit! She had made an amazing presence when she yelled them into silence and all her boldness had been ruined by the damn cough.

She took a sip of the water and sat calmly. "Thank you all for coming and I'm sorry to keep you waiting," she began, occasionally clearing her throat. "I invited everyone to this meeting because the secret leaked."

Surprised, they all stared at one another trying to figure out who leaked the secret.

"We agreed to protect this secret. I paid you to take the secret to your grave, but someone couldn't keep his mouth shut and now Raymond Brock's life is being hunted because someone has his eyes on the Connor Wealth," she said, her voice hardening. "I'm not saying any of you is involved in the conspiracy to end Raymond Brock's life. I am saying you might have told someone that told someone that told someone and that someone might be the one involve in this conspiracy." She paused for a while to make sure they understood her. "I need names of people you told. Husband, you told your wife about it. Please let me know. Fathers, you told your son, let me know. Who knows, your son might have told another person. That's why it's important that I know everyone you told."

"Stop right there!" Joe Connor said, glaring at Tamara. Joe was tall, almost as tall as Raymond. His slightly tanned skin blended with his sandy blond hair. His thick brow furrowed as he spoke. "There's a breach of agreement right here. We had an agreement! Raymond only controls Connor Corp as long as the secret doesn't leak that he is a Connor. We are trying to protect our father's image. His legacy. No one should know that he had an illegitimate child. And now that the secret is leaked, I think we should be talking about how to take Connor Corp away from Raymond."

"Stop right there! Let this be the last time you're going to ever talk as if you're doing Raymond a favor by letting him run Connor Corp. Because guess what? You aren't doing him no favor. He was self-sufficient, invincible. Your father needed him to look after his wealth. Your father couldn't leave his wealth in your hands because he knows you and your brother are irresponsible and you will squander the wealth. So he left everything for Raymond. Your father needed him! You both need him!" Tamara's expression turned more dangerous than his. Joe sat frozen, afraid to move, his eyes wide. "So next time before you say anything about taking back Connor Corp from Raymond, I want you to know that you are number one on my suspect list. You have so much to gain if Raymond dies that I wouldn't be surprise if you are at the center of this conspiracy. If you don't want my attention more than you already have, if you don't want me investigating your private affairs, then you should think twice about taking any selfish move!"

Joe swallowed hard and managed to give a weak nod.

"Good." The glare left her face, leaving calm again in its place. She withdrew her gaze from Joe and glanced around. "Like I said, I need names of people you told about Raymond being a Connor. His life depends on the names." She turned to Megan. "Megan, please, have them write down the names."

She glanced back at them. "Thank you all for coming. I appreciate you." Standing up from the armchair, she headed for the door. Hand on the doorknob, she halted as if something had struck her. Then she turned back at them. "I know most of you have dirty laundries. I won't be happy to show them to the public but I will if you refuse to tell the truth of how the secret leaked." She gave a sarcastic smile. "Please, make a wise decision as you write the names."

She finished and walked out of the room.

Chapter 19

Ever so gently, Tamara touched the tube to her lips and glided on the Matte red. She had always lacked the patient for lipstick and only used it on special occasion. But it was a special occasion—Bishop Shepherd had organized an event to celebrate the happiness in his home after several weeks of battle with anger, the press and some of his church members who felt disappointed.

The press had moved on to another story, the church members had forgiven him and the bishop had made a substantial improvement in managing his anger. There was peace in their home, the peace that had not been there in a long time. Peace that was worth celebrating.

Next, Tamara rubbed a translucent lip gloss as she smoothed her lips together. She drew back slightly to look at her reflection in the mirror and Tamara admitted that she liked the finished products.

She arrived at the event quite late, but that was alright because she didn't really like social events or gatherings like this.

Sophistication perfumed the event and Tamara caught many unfamiliar faces staring at her. Teetering in her heels, her hair bounced in signature curls with each movement. Her eyes quickly scanned the hall for any familiar face. Good for her, she noticed Sherry and Megan sitting far left of the room. Their eyes met and they smiled and gestured that she should come sit with them.

As she walked across the room to take a seat next to them, Bishop Shepherd took notice of her.

"Ladies and gentlemen," he said, raising his voice and pointing to her. "Tamara Price, the wonder woman that God used to restore the peace in my home."

Eyes shifted to her and the applause almost deafened her. Giving a humble smile, she bowed slightly.

"I must say Miss Price could be a hard nut to crack. She scolded me many times," he said with no malice in his voice. "But at the end, she fixed my marriage. Miss Price is a wonderful and amazing woman. I pray that God continues to strengthen her."

"Amen," everyone chorused.

They gave her another applause and she bowed slightly again, smiling. By the time the attention shifted away from her, she continued to walk to find a seat near Megan and Sherry. When she lifted her face, her eyes miraculously singled out Raymond among the crowd and their gaze met. Her heart pounded in her chest. She felt a tightening in the pit of her stomach.

What the heck was he doing at the event? She had managed to avoid him since the night of their passionate lovemaking. To stare at his devilishly handsome face this night made her quivered. Millions of emotions clashed through her. Goosebumps rose up her skin as the hair stood on its end.

She wasn't ready yet. She wasn't ready to look him in the face and explain why she claimed the other night meant nothing to her.

She glanced at his direction again. Their eyes met again. And then he stood up, as if he was coming for her.

Her breath caught in her throat for an instant. Very quickly, she turned around and hurried out of the event hall. As she walked out of the hall, she heard footsteps behind her. Sucking in her breath, she increased her pace. She got out of the building. If she could get to her car, she would just drive off very quickly, she thought. She had made appearance at the event already. There was no need to stay any longer.

His footsteps followed more quickly than she imagined. In a twinkle of an eye, he caught up with her, grabbed her by the arm and drew her close.

Tamara yanked her arm away from his hold. "What?"

He didn't respond. Hands in his pockets, he stood still, gazing at her.

His gaze turned her into a melting candle. She took few steps away before the fire radiating from him would melt the whole of her, before she would run into his arms and kiss him.

"What do you want?" she asked, her voice almost gentle.

Taking two gentle steps closer to Tamara, he took his hands out of his pocket. "No, Mara. You should tell me what it is you want. You can't jump into bed with me one minute and the next you're piercing my heart with a sword," he said, not taking his eyes off her for a second. "Tell me, Mara, what is it you want?"

Trying not to betray any emotion, Tamara met his gaze. "I want things to go back to the way they were before."

"This is the way it was," he replied with a painful smile. "We attend events together. We are always together. Our eyes find each other amidst a thousand people. And when we are alone, we make sweet, great passionate love. We connect. We get along. We joke. We laugh. We play. We love. That is us!"

She shivered. His words had become a wind of emotions blowing through her, reminding her of the old times. Taking another two steps backward, she shook her head gently. "I mean the way it was before that night at my place. I want us to go back to the time when we barely talk, when we barely look at each other, when we don't care about each other."

"There was never a time a like that. There was never a time we don't care about each other."

"Ray, there was. Before that night, it was like that."

"This is all about that night."

It wasn't even a question.

But she answered anyway.

"Yes. It's about that night." She glared at his face. "Do you know how much it's killing me that I slept with you?"

Raymond pulled his brows together in a frown. "What?"

She nodded, raising her voice. "Yes. Because you're married to my best friend. My client! You're not the right person for me. You're already taken. You're married." Tears gathered in the corner of her eyes and she feared that she might cry. Quickly, she turned to leave, rushing to her car.

"So this is about Dahlia, right?"

"No!" she yelled as she turned back and walked back to where Raymond stood. "This isn't about Dahlia." She stood right in front of him, gazing into his brown eyes in the near darkness. He looked pained. But she was in pain too. Tears ran down her cheeks in brooks. When he didn't say anything, she decided she'd be honest with him.

"She was my client. I promised to help her save her marriage. I smile at her, encourage her, all the while desperately hoping that her marriage will end." She was crying, but her voice was steady and harder than she had intended. "I wanted the marriage to end because I want to be with you. Because no matter how much you hurt me, my heart still beats for you. I can't get over you. I flirt with you, make out with you and open my laps for you while I kept promising her that I would save her marriage. And that makes me a bad person compared to Dahlia. Because when she took you from me, we weren't married. But now, you're married to her. You own her and she owns you and…"

"Dahlia doesn't own me. You own me!" he cut her off, yelling with tears in his voice. "When I'm with Dahlia, you're always on my mind. When she sits next to me, I don't even see her. I see you. You don't have to remind me that I'm married. I know, but I'm in love with you. I love you. You're my heartbeat. My heart beats for you. My heart is with you. My heart belongs to you. The whole of me belongs to you. And I don't regret what happened that night. Not for a second. So don't just stand there and give me that lecture about who is good or bad. Because when it comes to you, nothing else matters to me. Only you matters, Mara. Only you."

He stared at her earnestly, his brown eyes never more beautiful than that moment.

Tears flooding her face, she just wanted to walk over and run into his arms. Before she could, Raymond stopped her with his strong hands holding on her upper arms, looking at her face.

"But I won't force myself on you. If you don't want to see me again, I'll understand. I'll leave now and never bother you again. And I want you to be with me because you want to. If you get in the car with me and leave with me this night, it's because you're convinced that you won't regret it. You're free to do whatever, walk away or go with me. But know this, Mara, I want you to choose me and go with me. I want you, Mara, more than anything. More than the Connor wealth. More than life itself because I can't breathe without you."

She stood there in front of him, tears running down her cheeks with her heart breaking all over again.

"Please, Mara," he pleaded. "Come with me."

She shivered slightly at the imagination of what might lie ahead if she did. She couldn't think straight. She didn't even want to let herself think too deeply about it. She didn't know what her choice would be. But she could feel it.

She looked at him, deep into his eyes.

And she was certain of what she wanted.

She nodded and smiled slightly.

Crashing into his arms, she buried her wet face in his chest as the sob racked through her body.

His car was parked few strides away. Slowly, they walked to his car. He opened the passenger seat for her. She got in while he slipped into the driver seat. He glanced at her and smile.

Tamara leaned her head against the leather seat. "Where are we going?"

A grin covered his face. "Rhode Island, baby."

Tamara stared wide-eyed. "What?"

He leaned over, wiped a tear from her face and placed a soft, tiny kiss on her lips. Then he leaned back into the driver seat and they were off.

Chapter 20

"You're joking, right?" Tamara asked. "We're not going to Rhode Island."

"Yes, we are. I have some urgent business in Rhode Island."

Tamara rolled her eyes.

He slowed down and looked over at her, smiling. "C'mon, Mara, it's only a six hours drive from Baltimore to Rhode Island. We'll be back tomorrow evening."

"You know, some other billionaire would have run their business errands using a private jet."

"I'm not some other billionaire. I wasn't born a billionaire. I was born normal and I want to live normal because I like normal. Besides, I like the road. And stop talking as if you don't like the roads 'cause I know you do."

She nodded, smiling. "Of course, I do love the road. You remember our trip to Vegas?"

He laughed. "Yeah. Yeah. I remember. At Marquee club, you got into a drinking competition with me..."

She interrupted. "I was so drunk..."

"And then you got up to use the ladies' room only to end up falling into the trash can."

She laughed, made her palm into a fist and hit his shoulder playfully. "I fell beside the trash can. Not into the trash can."

He laughed back. "Beside the trash can and into the trash, it's the same."

"And everyone was watching and laughing. And you had to come to my aid and carry me to the car."

He nodded, laughing.

"And I remember the LA trip, too," she said.

"Oh! No, no no. Please, don't talk about that," he pleaded, clearly embarrassed.

"Your lips turned red and swelled up huge because you were allergic to something in the food we ate. And you had to walk around with a napkin covering your mouth."

He laughed. "I remember the trip to Texas."

"And New Orleans," she said.

"And New Jersey. That was one sweet, hilarious trip!"

Tamara's laugh slowly became a gentle smile. "You were right. We're always together."

His laugh became a tight little smile. "Yeah. I know," he said in a low voice.

The memory of everything returned to her and she just couldn't help herself: she broke down in tears.

She knew she was being too emotional, but she couldn't help it.

He slammed on the brakes and looked at her with those beautiful eyes of his. "What? Did I say something? Did I hurt you?"

She shook her head.

"What's wrong?"

"I didn't think a moment like this could still come." She fought back the sobs. "I...I miss us."

He leaned closer and held her wet face in both hands and kissed her. Gently. Softly. Tenderly.

Then he pulled back and still holding her face and staring into her eyes, he wiped a tear from her face.

"I'm sorry," he whispered. "For everything."

She nodded slightly and smiled sadly.

He leaned closer to kiss her again.

Before he could, a car beeped its horn behind them.

Staring into his eyes, she said, "Guess we have to go."

He considered for a while. "No. He can wait."

Leaning over, he kissed her again. They were lost in the kiss until the beeping horn almost deafened them.

They finally broke the kiss with a laugh.

Tamara pulled away, smiling. "Someone is going to smash your car from behind."

He smiled. "I know."

He started the engine and continued the journey.

Few minutes later, Tamara relaxed her back and yawned.

"Tilt the seat back and sleep," he said.

Tamara did as she was told. "Hey, driver," she yawned. "Wake me up when we get to Rhode Island."

He smiled. "Yes, ma'am."

Tamara closed her eyes, but wasn't totally asleep yet. Few minutes into the journey, she felt Raymond grabbed her hand. He held it close to his chest and squeezed it tight... Then he held it to his lips and kissed it over and over again.

Tamara pretended to be asleep. But maybe it was how much emotions Raymond had shown that night, or how he was so opened and honest about his feelings for her. All that she knew was that she felt so relieved as if all her sadness had suddenly turned into joy.

****

Tamara woke up and sat up. The first morning of ray of sunlight flashed into Tamara's eyes. It was around 6:00 a.m.

"It's morning," she said. She had only intended to take a short nap and she had slept throughout the night.

"Welcome to Rhode Island, sleepyhead," Raymond replied.

"You drove throughout the night?"

"Yes, baby."

She yawned and tried to stretch her hands and legs. "I told you to wake me up when we get here."

"I wanted to get to the hotel before waking you up."

Tamara stared out through the window. "It's beautiful."

"Yes, it's beautiful. You've not been here

before?"

"Yeah," Tamara replied, still staring out through the window.

"Well, I planned that we'd go back to Baltimore this night. But it's okay if you want to stay one more day to actually tour the city."

She glanced back at Raymond. "Really? Can I? You have a very busy schedule…"

"Yes. You can. Don't worry about my schedule."

"Awwww…" She leaned over and gave him a quick kiss. "You're a darling."

A grin covered his handsome face.

Tamara reached for her purse and grabbed her cell phone. "I need to call Drake and let him know I wouldn't be coming to work today."

Raymond nodded. "Ok."

Tamara placed a call to Drake. It didn't ring for long when he picked the call.

"You're not sleeping?" Tamara asked.

Drake replied, "I'm at work. I decided to come in early. Please, come over to work as fast as you can. We should handle this together. It's important."

"I'm out of town. I'm not in Baltimore right now."

"What? You didn't say anything about going out of town."

"It came impromptu. I'm sorry," she apologized. "Drake, I left my car at the event hall last night. Would you please go pick it for me? I don't want it to get towed."

"No Probs. I'll pick it up today. Where's your

spare key?"

"The usual place."

"Alright."

"Thanks."

"So what took you out of town?" Drake asked.

Tamara looked over at Raymond and smiled. "I went to Rhode Island with Raymond."

"Raymond? You mean you went all the way to the Island just to get laid," Drake said with humor in his voice.

"Drake!!!" Tamara warned.

"Damn! I need to get laid too."

"Good. So go to your girlfriend."

"I don't have a girlfriend."

"Then go to your secret girlfriend."

"She broke up with me."

"Then move to your secret secret girlfriend."

"That would be you."

"Drake, shut up!" she said and tried to change the subject. "So what happened? Why are you at work early?"

"Tamara, we checked the Brock's apartment. It was clean."

Tamara raised a brow. "What do you mean it's clean?"

"We found nothing. It was as if someone on the inside told her we were coming. We didn't find anything that could be a weapon. No poison or chemical like we thought, no guns, not even a harmless kitchen knife."

"How could it be? She threatened to kill Raymond." She took a quick look at Raymond. With the look on his face, she was certain he wasn't happy about being the topic of discussion.

"Well we didn't find nothing," Drake said. "So I came in early to read through the names written down by the 15. None of them confessed that they told Dahlia anything about Raymond being a Connor."

"Keep looking at the names and try to find out who those people are. One of them might know Dahlia. However, I'm still certain that Dahlia is planning to kill Raymond and if she's going to do it, it's going to be through poison. I'm going to try and convince Raymond to get a toxin test. I'll be back by tomorrow and we'll think of the next step of action. But if anything comes up, I'm only a phone call away."

"Okay."

She hung up.

"Don't ask," Raymond said. "I'm not testing for toxin."

Tamara frowned. "Is it possible that you want to die? Because this is not the reaction I was expecting."

"I told you to stay out of this. I will handle it. I told you that, didn't I?"

Tamara's frown deepened. "And I remember telling you that I will not stay out of it."

At that moment, Raymond pulled up at parking lot of Hotel Providence. "Mara, this is bigger and more dangerous than you think," he said, his voice very gentle. "I won't forgive myself if any harm comes to you."

Raymond got out of the car and held open the passenger door. Tamara stepped out of the car too, holding tightly to her purse. "Don't worry about me..." she stopped talking when a stranger passed by her. They both feign a smile in greeting to him. When he was gone, Tamara continued, "Don't worry about me being safe. I can take care of myself."

"So it's okay for you to say you can take care of yourself, but it's not okay for me to tell you that I can take care of this and you don't need to get involve."

"Raymond, all you have to do is take the toxin test and prove me wrong."

"Stay out of it, Mara."

"Dahlia gave a death threat. She threatened to kill you and you expect me to just do nothing?"

"Trust me, I know Dahlia. She's not capable of that. She received instructions to kill me one year ago. If she hasn't done it till now, that means she's not capable," he said, his voice a little higher than a whisper.

"One year? What...?" She stopped talking as they finally got to the reception, her hand in his. They both feign a smile to the receptionist. She smiled back and welcomed them. When she was done processing their reservation, she handed them the key card and with a big bright smile, she told them to enjoy their stay.

Immediately they left the front desk, she leaned closer to him and continued the conversation, keeping her voice low. "She received her instructions from who? How did you get to know?"

He pressed the elevator button and they

waited. "Well..."

Before he could say further, the elevator opened and they walked in. Tamara felt his arms around her waist as he drew her close. "Times like this, I think you're in the wrong profession. You should be a detective, not a lawyer."

Tamara gave a sideway glance, made her palm into a fist and playfully hit him. "There, don't you think I should be a boxer and not a lawyer?"

He gave a low laugh. "Yes, if you love to get beaten."

She smiled and hit him again.

Chapter 21

Raymond knew how inquisitive Tamara could be. He knew if there was anything that was consistent about Tamara, it was that she hated when her questions received no answers. He'd love to give an answer to her question, but giving an answer would mean they'd have to talk about Dahlia. And he hated it. Because Dahlia was the reason he ruined everything in the first place.

The elevator stopped at their floor and Raymond pulled the key card out of his pocket and opened the door. As soon as he walked into the room, he shrugged of his suit jacket, loosened the first three buttons of his shirt and he relaxed himself on the neatly made up bed.

Tamara crept into bed with him, placing her head on his chest and caressing it.

Raymond felt her body tightened in anticipation of his touch. Arms around her, he sucked in a breath, inhaling the warm fragrance of her in his arms.

Slowly, she raised her head from his chest and brought her face very close to his. She kissed him.

Her lips were so soft yet sweet. The kiss was so magical it threatened to start up a fire of passion within him. As their lips locked together, he felt different. As if the future flashed before his eyes and he saw that she was his happiness.

She pulled away very slowly.

Face so close together, he kept staring at her with his eyes naked with emotions.

"You're staring at me," she said in a whisper.

Eyes still fixed on her, he said in a low, sexy voice, "you don't like being stared at, try not to be so beautiful."

She smiled, almost shyly. "I tried, but can't seem to help it."

She wasn't expecting it, but he pulled her face closer and kissed her, angling his head to make the kiss deeper. He felt himself stir into hardness as the fire of desire burnt through him.

And then she pulled away very gently. "Who gave Dahlia the order to kill you? How did you know..."

"Ah, Mara. Please, don't use that tactic," he pleaded.

She brought her face so close he could feel her breath. Her lips were almost touching his and for a second, he thought she'd kiss him again. But she didn't.

"What tactic, Ray?" she asked, slowly licking her lips.

"This tactic," he replied, humor in his voice. "Arousing me to get info from me. It's extortion."

"No. It's not extortion. Even if it is, you still have to tell me."

"Mara."

Her expression turned deadly serious. "Why is it so difficult for you to just answer my question? What are you hiding?"

He swallowed, his only answer a sigh.

Tamara stood up from the bed. Her cheeks flushed as the blood inside her began to boil. "Last night, you gave that big speech about how much you love me. And only few hours later, you're hiding things from me already."

Still lying on the bed, he patted the bed next to him. "Come over here and let's talk."

Tamara hesitated.

"Mara, come here," he growled in a deep, firm voice.

Cautiously, she crawled and sat next to him on the bed. He held her arm and pulled her to himself, placing her head on his chest and raising her face up so he could see her face. "I am not hiding anything from you. It's difficult for me to answer your question because there's no way I can actually answer your question without telling you what actually went down between myself and Dahlia. And you've made it clear to me that you don't want to know."

"I don't want to know," she said, stood up from the bed and walked toward the bathroom. "I need a shower."

Raymond caught up with her and threw himself in front of her, preventing her from opening the door. "Why?" he asked. "Why didn't you want to know?"

"Because..." she stopped, suddenly finding it

difficult to say the words. "Because I...I'm not sure if I'll be able to forgive it."

Holding her upper arm, he drew her to himself. He raised a hand to her face, using a finger to gently brush off the strand of hair on her face. "Mara, it's going to be difficult to have a fresh start if you don't know..."

Mara smiled. Trying desperately to change the topic, she interrupted him by raising her face to meet his and kissed him. She was only planning on kissing him, to make him change the topic, but once her lips were connected with his, she couldn't stop herself.

Their kiss grew intense.

It had been a rough night for Tamara. Too rough. However, as Raymond pushed her against the bathroom door, fervently kissing her, she knew that this day would at least have a happy beginning.

She moaned into the kiss, only to have him begin sucking on her bottom lip. She wrapped her long, black arms around his neck as he lifted her from the ground, cupping her rear for support. Raymond brought his lips downward, peppering her neck with small kisses. She let out a tiny whimper as she felt his teeth meet her soft smooth skin, knowing there would be a mark there later, but also realizing that she didn't give a damn.

His left hand found its way beneath her short, black dress and to her hot pink lace panties. She bit her bottom lip, trying to hold back the whine of pleasure that shot through her spine like electricity as his strong, rough hands caressed her entrance. Sweat beaded down her forehead as she felt heat rushing through her body, forcing her to grind against his hand, writhing in anticipation, wanting that release.

Raymond could feel her moisten beneath his fingers, smirking somewhat as she bucked against him, purring with lust. He felt an arm being removed from his neck, and moved to the button of the dark trousers that he wore. He could feel her fingers fumble with the button, drunk with frustration and desire, but soon enough he felt the satisfying snap. The constricting fabric encasing his legs was gone in a flash.

Tamara quickly unzipped Raymond's pants, pulling them, along with his boxers, down artfully with one hand. She instantly wrapped her fingers around his hard and growing member, stroking it with as much consistency as she could manage. She smiled devilishly as it elicited a deep groan of pleasure from the man, and jerked her hand faster.

Raymond could not concentrate on littering the stunning woman before him with kisses anymore. No, with the things that she was doing to him, he couldn't hold back any longer. He swiftly removed her from the bathroom door, and sat her on the center table. Raymond slipped the panties (which he happened to notice as being pink) down her silky legs, and passed the six inch black stilettos that she still wore.

She inhaled sharply when he pushed inside of

her, but somehow remained breathless. Her head fell back, letting her dark hair flow onto the table. He filled her completely, making her want to scream bloody murder, but only able to moan as he thrust in and out. His pace was slow, and it was like torture. She pushed against him, using her hips and it was his turn to gasp.

He slipped a hand up her dress, using it to grab one of her perfectly shaped breasts, using his thumb to toy with the erect nipple. She wheezed at the movement and began to grind harder against him. Raymond quickly slipped the straps of her dress from her shoulders, instantly revealing her rigid nipples and a chest drenched in sweat. He pressed his lips to her right breast, sucking on it.

Tamara let out a shout as Raymond bit down on her breast, and then followed it with a moan. His large, strong hands gripped the other one, sending a crash of delight coursing through her bones. She needed more.

When he realized that Tamara's pace was far quicker than his, he grunted and flipped her over, so that her chest was flat on the table. Raymond snaked his hands around her waist, using it to pull himself in and out of her faster.

"Ohhh" barely escaped her lips as she held onto the edges of the table as his thrusts grew quicker and stronger. The table shook wildly, causing the vase of flowers to fall off with a definite crash. That was of no importance to Tamara, as the sensation of being filled was sharper than ever. Her moans quickly turned to shouts as he steadily forced into her, the slapping of his hips against her butt only furthering that. After a few moments, all she could see was stars as he pushed into her, completely unaware that her shouts had turned into screams.

The sensation rippled through her as he growled loudly and released his load into her, and in one final moment of utter bliss, she screamed, arching her back as she did, her hair plastered to her skin from sweat. She fell against the table, debilitated by the fading waves of ecstasy, as he did the same, collapsing to the side of her.

"That was good, right?" she asked, panting in labored breath.

Trying to catch his breath, he said, "Good? That was awesome."

He drew her in, kissing her tenderly— a silent 'thank you' and they remained like that for an immeasurable amount of time, just a panting, sweaty heap on the table.

Chapter 22

Tamara glanced around. "We broke the vase. The hotel..."

Raising a shoulder in a shrug, he interrupted her. "We can replace it."

"For a second right there I forgot my boyfriend is a billionaire," she said, shrieking as he pounced and tickled her.

He ended the tickling with a slow, long kiss and they lay in each other's arms for a while.

Then Raymond stood. "We need a shower." He pulled her along with him, leading the way to the bathroom.

When Tamara saw the Jacuzzi tub, she quickly changed her mind. "I think I want a bath instead."

"That's okay."

He turned on the faucet for the Jacuzzi tub and water spewed out and began to fill up the bathtub.

"Hold on, I'll be back in a sec," he said and left the bathroom.

Tamara waited for a while. But when she

began to hear his voice, seems like he was talking on phone. She decided she'd wait for him in the tub.

Tamara eased herself into the bubbly water with a hint of steam coming from it. She relaxed instantaneously as the warmness hit her skin. It was a soothing feeling, as she already felt that she would be sore for a few days to come. She closed her eyes and sunk into the salt-infused water, ready to drift away.

A few moments later, however, she heard the distinct splash of water. Her eyes fluttered open, just in time to be greeted by the pleasant sight of Raymond. She pushed off of her side and squeezed next to him, enjoying the smooth, steady beat of his heart as he wrapped his arm around her.

He shifted up, removing his arm, and beckoned for her to sit up.

Raymond reached for the bath sponge hanging off of the bar in the shower, and for a bar of fancy soap. He turned her around, and began gently scrubbing her back.

She giggled as he did so, the sensation of the fabric on her back tickling her ever so slightly. He then rinsed the suds off, and she turned back to him. He was smiling smugly— almost as if he was proud of his work.

"Let me do you," she said, and he obliged happily. Though the sex had been nice (hell, it had been fantastic), these moments of tender affection that they shared was what really warmed the cackles of her heart. She sighed dreamily, thankful for the man in front of her.

She worked up lather and ran her sudsy hands over his chest, his arms, his neck. When her hands went to his thighs, she felt his erection. She giggled.

"You caused that," he said.

She washed it very quickly and took her hands off it.

Raymond shook his head with a naughty smile. "No. Not clean enough."

"Ray!" she said, smiling. She went back to his erection, washed it and massage it a little longer.

"Unh…" he grunted, closing his eyes.

"Clean enough now?"

He winked at her. "Yes, baby."

When they both exited the bath, Raymond pulled her in for a kiss which she accepted without hesitation, the overgrown stubble on his face causing a prickly sensation.

"You should probably shave again pretty soon. You're getting pretty scruffy," she said, wrapping a light blue towel around her waist.

"And what if I like being scruffy?" he mumbled. She rolled her eyes playfully and pulled him toward the sink, sitting him down on the edge of the drained porcelain tub.

"Well if you won't, I will," she said playfully, obtaining a pink disposable razor from the cabinet and vanilla-scented shaving cream.

One of his eyebrows cocked upward in semi horror. "You know what I think I can handle it."

"No, I insist." She cackled wildly, just to strike the fear of god into Raymond.

She applied the cream and began shaving; quickly realizing that it was a lot more difficult to do on someone else.

She tried to be as careful as she could, but ended up cutting him every once in a while. It was safe to say that he would have been better off looking a little scruffy. However, Raymond took it in stride, and didn't complain about it too much. He was able to be with the woman he longed for, and that was worth more than a few measly cuts.

They got into the shower and wash off and when they exit the shower, Raymond leaned in to give her a gentle kiss. "Now to the room. I need a little rest before attending the meeting I came for."

"You go ahead. I want to do few clean up. I'll join you."

He kissed her again. "Okay baby."

Immediately he walked out of the bathroom, Tamara reached for the razor. Raymond might think Dahlia wasn't capable of hurting him, but she believed Dahlia was more than capable. And she was going to get him tested without his consent.

Putting the razor in a Ziploc bag, she hid it in the cabinet. She would take the razor with her back to Baltimore and get it tested for toxins. She secretly hoped that Raymond would be right, that the test would come back negative, that Dahlia was in fact not capable of poisoning him.

She waited a while and then she opened the door and walked into the room. "Ray, we don't have a change of clothes."

****

When Raymond walked out of the bathroom, room service came to deliver the clothes and shoes he'd ordered for himself and Tamara before he went into the bath. He took the clothes and tipped the room service $400 for the stress.

He arranged the new clothes on the bed. He placed Tamara's panties separate and then the top and dress-up pants. He was about to put on his suit trousers when his phone rang. He took a quick look at the phone to see who it was. It was Joe Connor, his brother.

He picked the call, thinking why the heck is Joe calling him? "Hello, bro," he said.

"Ray, where are you?"

"Providence, Rhode Island. What's the prob, Joe?"

"Have you listened to the news today?"

"No. What's wrong? What's the prob.?" Raymond asked.

"Ray, I don't know how to tell you. So go ahead and look up the internet. When you're done, hit me back."

"Okay."

Raymond hung up.

Quickly, he opened his browser and look up the day's news.

Raymond Brock, illegitimate son of the late James Connor and CEO of Connor Corp revealed. And his affair with the supposed marriage fixer, Tamara Price.

Hot sweat covered him and he stopped

reading. Pictures of Tamara and him were everywhere on the internet. He recognized some of the pictures. One of them was him and Tamara walking into the hotel this morning. Another was the moment he was holding Tamara in his arms the previous night.

Who did this? Who leaked the story to the press? Why did they have to drag Tamara into this? It's going to ruin her, ruin the career she'd built all these years. His heart heaved in his chest as he racked his brain thinking on what to do next.

His phone rang and disrupted his thoughts.

Picking the call, Raymond said, "Hello…"

"Raymond CONNOR!!! You're fired!!!" the caller said, and then hung up.

That was his boss at MDNC. Raymond understood his anger perfectly and his reason for firing him. He had lied, kept working for him and kept receiving the peanut salary when in fact he could afford to buy off the TV station.

His phone rang again.

"I got the news, Joe," Raymond said.

"What are you going to do? I think you should stay in Providence till everything goes away. Trust me, the press will move to another story very soon and they'll forget about you and Tamara."

"No. No. I can't just hide in the face of all the scandal. That's not the right thing to do. I'm coming back to Baltimore immediately."

"Are you sure your woman is going to be okay with this idea?"

"Mara is a fighter. I know her. She's a strong woman. She's going to be okay with it."

"Alright then, bro. I'll send a private jet to come get you."

"No, Joe. I'll have Anita schedule my flight."

"Okay. Let me know immediately you land. I'll have bodyguards waiting to escort you to Connor Corps."

"Thanks Joe."

"Anything for you, bro."

Raymond hung up and placed a quick call to Anita.

"Hello, Sir,"

"Don't Sir me, Anita," Raymond replied. "My guess is you heard the news too."

"Yes, Sir."

"You are still my PA, right?"

"If you want me to quit MDNC and work for you, I'll be more than willing, Sir."

"You're hired. Go ahead and schedule me on a flight from Providence to Baltimore. Two first class seat for me and Tamara. Get it done within the hour."

"Okay Sir."

"Thanks," Raymond said.

Before he could hang up, he heard Anita spoke. "But, sir, we haven't talked about the terms of payment."

"Anita!!!" he growled, and then he hung up.

Almost immediately, Tamara's phone rang. Raymond checked to see who it was. It was Drake. Raymond knew what the call would be about, but if Tamara had to know about it, she had to hear it from him first.

The bathroom door opened and Tamara walked to the room. "Ray, we don't have a change of clothes."

"Really? Take a second look at the bed."

"You ordered us new clothes." She sat on the bed, taking a good look at the clothes. "I love it. You know exactly what I like." She gave him a quick hug and then a small kiss. "Thanks baby."

"You're welcome."

"How did you get this done?"

"I had help from a lady who works here."

"Awww. Did you reward her?"

"I gave her $400."

"What? That's too much. $400 could buy me a shoe."

He stifled a laugh. "Mara!"

Chapter 23

Raymond made sure that Tamara was done putting on her clothes before he began gently, "Mara, we need to talk!"

When a man suddenly says 'we need to talk', a heart is probably about to be broken, Tamara thought.

Raymond saw uneasiness took over her once relaxed face. "No, it's not what you're thinking." He held her and helped her sit on the bed.

"The secret is out!" he said.

She jumped to her feet. "Which of them? That you are James Connor's son?"

Raymond nodded slowly.

Tamara began to pace back and forth. Hot air rose within her and she felt stuffy. Her brain was thinking about a million things at the same time, trying to process everything, trying to think of a solution.

"And..."

She cut him off. "They know you're the one controlling Connor Corp."

He nodded. "Yes. My boss at MDNC just fired

me."

"No! No!" she yelled, still pacing.

"And they know about us too," Raymond added solemnly.

His words brought her to a halt. She tried to tell herself to be calm. Breathe in. Breathe out. Breathe in. Breathe out.

And then she sat back down on the bed. She turned to look at him, tears in her eyes. "Ray, this is not good for you."

"What do you mean? I'm not a celebrity. The public don't care about who or who is not running Connor Corp."

"The board of directors is going to question your personality. Most people on the board see themselves as saints. If they find out you're having extra-marital affair…"

He cut her off. "I'm worried about you. This is going to ruin your reputation. You're supposed to fix people's marriage and…"

"I'm screwing my client's husband," she said. Sucking in her breath, she held her face in her palm. "What am I going to do?" Tears ran down her cheeks.

"What are we going to do?" he corrected. Putting an arm around her, he drew her closer. "We're in this together." He held her in his arms a while. Then he held her wet face in his palm and kissed her. "We're going to get through this. Okay?"

She nodded slowly.

"Ray, promise me one thing."

With his thumb, he wiped a tear from her

face. "What, baby?"

"That whatever happens, you're going to be on my side."

"There's no side here, Mara," he said, looking into her eyes. "It's just you and me. Together. Till the end. Okay?"

She nodded. "Okay."

"So let's go back to Baltimore. We need to go sort things out."

****

It's a one hour flight from Providence, RI to Baltimore, MD. Security team waited at the airport for them, shielding them from the paparazzi.

As the Bentley Limo pulled up at the parking lot of Tamara's office building, Raymond took her hands in his. "You know how I feel about you, right?"

She nodded.

"Okay. Know that whatever happens, that feeling will never change."

She nodded again.

"And we are in this together. Okay?"

"Okay."

And then he gave her a slow, long, lingering kiss. And Tamara stepped out of the car.

When Tamara walked into the conference room, all eyes shifted to her.

"Tamara, you've got to see this," Sherry said. She took the TV remote control and increased the volume.

Tamara's eyes caught her own image on the TV and she tried to pay attention.

That woman paid her to help fix her marriage and instead of doing her job, she was having an affair the woman's husband. I sure as hell can never trust such a woman with my marriage. Hell no, can't trust her with my man.

I was once Tamara's client. I knew I caught her seducing my husband. I just wasn't sure at that time. But now, I'm more than certain.

We kept praising this woman that she saves marriages. We never question her methods.

If she is so good at saving marriages, why is she still single? I mean, you will expect someone like her to be happily married.

Thank God that woman's secret is exposed. This will be a lesson to all women to be careful and stop running to just about anybody asking for help with their marriage. Whatever issues you got with your man, fix it yourself. You don't need no marriage fixer to fix it for you.

Tamara's head was spinning. Her heart broke a thousand times over. Everyone she had ever helped, they were all on the TV talking her down. She had fought for them again and again. And none of them fought for her. She had stood up for them, and none of them would do the same for her. No one was on her side. Most of them had cheated on their spouses, she didn't judge them. She just helped them. And none of them tried to understand her, they just judged her.

Drake took the TV remote control and turned down the volume. "We've lost more than ten clients since the news broke. They all withdrew their cases from us."

Tears gathered in her eyes. And she hurried out of the conference room before she could cry.

But then they all stood up and followed her.

She wanted them to give her a little privacy so that she can cry her eyes out.

As she sat on the armchair in her office, her head ached due to the tears she had been holding back. Few seconds later, the desk phone rang.

She picked up the receiver. "Tamara Price. How may I help you?"

"It's Tiffany. I just want you to know that I'm highly disappointed in you."

"Tiffany, there's an explanation..."

Before she could say further, the caller hung up.

Slowly, she dropped the receiver. Her eyes cautiously went to meet Megan, Sherry and Drake's gaze. And then she smiled sadly. "Don't screw a client! The rules I set for our law firm, I was the first to break it."

"Ah! Tamara," Drake said, emotions evident in his voice.

The desk phone rang again.

"Don't!" Drake said.

"I have to." Tamara replied and picked up the receiver.

"Tamara Price & Associates, how may I help you?"

"I'm calling to let you know that I don't want you handling my case anymore. I don't want you screwing my husband."

Before she could respond, the caller dropped the call.

Tears ran down her cheeks. How could people be so mean, rude and heartless?

Drake tried to move closer to her.

She raised a palm to gesture him not to.

Her cell phone rang. She checked to see who it was.

Her mother.

She pressed the green button and slowly pressed the phone to her ear. "Momma, go ahead and say it," she said.

"Say what, my dear?" her mother asked.

"That you're disappointed in me. That I let you down. Go ahead and preach to me about how wrong I am."

"No, baby. I was going to say that I understand you."

Tears rushed down her cheeks again. "Thanks, momma. It means a lot to me."

"I understand you, my baby. We all make mistakes and we all pay a price. Don't let what people say get to you; you're going to get through this. Okay?"

"Okay."

For the next few seconds, no one said anything.

Silence roared into her ears.

And then her mother broke the silence. "Are you going to be alright?"

"Yes."

"If you want to come and stay in my place for the moment…"

"I'll be alright, momma."

"Ok. Take care."

Tamara ended the call. The pain in her heart deepened and she felt like crawling into the bed, cover herself with her blanket and staying that way for days until everything would be over.

But she knew she couldn't afford to crash down like that. She needed to make this problem go away. Raymond needed her, too.

Very quickly, she wiped her tears, grabbed her purse, took the razor and handed it to Drake. "Please, take this to the lab and have them test it for toxins."

"Yes, boss."

"And we need to find out who leaked the story."

Sherry cut her off. "We don't need to bother about who leaked the story. I think we should be trying to put our own side of the story out there."

"I don't rush into battle without knowing who I'm fighting!" Tamara replied. "So, which news channel broke the story first?"

"MDNC," Drake replied.

Tamara grabbed her cell phone and began to search through the contact list on her cell phone.

"What are you gonna do?" Sherry asked.

"I have a friend in MDNC. Let's hope she will be willing to tell me who gave them the story."

For the next few minutes, Tamara was talking on phone, persuading the friend to tell her who gave them the story. Immediately Tamara dropped the call, her anger rose.

Tamara looked at Sherry, surprise and anger

flickering in her eyes. "What have you done?!" she yelled.

Megan's jaw dropped.

"What? Sherry?" Drake questioned, unable to believe the accusation.

Sherry glanced at their accusing faces. "I didn't mean to," she tried to explain. "Dahlia was blackmailing me. She was going to tell on me that I got admitted into the Law school using a fake undergrad transcript. I love the law and Dahlia was going to take it from me. I didn't have a choice."

"You had a choice!" Tamara yelled. "You could have told me."

The room was dead silent for the next few minutes. Tamara was pacing back and forth. Her brain was working so hard that it felt as if her head would explode.

"What else?" She stopped pacing. "What else have you told Dahlia? What else have you done for Dahlia?"

"I told Dahlia that we were going to search their home. That's the reason we found nothing when we went searching."

Tamara folded her arms across her chest, her gaze intense. "You're fired! Until Drake can confirm if your story is true, if Dahlia was actually blackmailing you or you're working for her."

"Tamara, please!"

Tamara ignored her plea.

Chapter 24

Raymond was welcomed with rivers of tears flowing out of Dahlia's eyes.

"You and Tamara. Is it true?"

Damn! He was in no mood for Dahlia's drama right now. He needed to clear his mind, think about how to rescue Tamara from the hell she was probably going through. Since the news of their affair broke, people had been judging her without trying to understand her for a second.

Hot rage shot through him. But he had learned long ago that the world wasn't always pretty or fair. Stuff happened. People who praise you will also talk you down should anything go wrong. That's the human nature.

Ignoring Dahlia, he walked past her and went to the couch.

Dahlia followed, sitting next to him. "Raymond. Tell me, you and Tamara, is it true?"

He nodded slightly.

Slowly, she relaxed her back, looking up at the ceiling. "I suck at being a wife, right? You had to go back to Tamara."

The room was dead silent for a second.

Dahlia swallowed hard and continued, "I'm trying, Raymond. I'm trying to be a good wife but you don't even care that I'm trying. You don't talk to me. You hide things from me. I didn't even know that you are James Connor's son. Imagine how I felt when I heard it on the news today."

Raymond let out a breath of exasperation. "Dahlia. Stop the lies, please. You've always known about my relationship with James Connor. That was the reason you married me in the first place."

"Ah! Raymond. How could you say that?"

Raymond sighed again. He didn't want to have this conversation. At all.

For one long second they were quiet again.

Dahlia sat closer, placed a hand on Raymond shoulder. "I know that you are angry and you are treating me this way because of what I did," she said, her voice very gentle. "And I'm sorry. But you've had your revenge on me. You had an affair with Tamara and now we are equal. Please, Raymond, you've punished me enough. Let's start again. Let's make this marriage work for the sake of our son."

Before Raymond could respond, the doorbell rang.

Dahlia stood from the couch and walked cautiously to the door to check who it was. "It's Joe Connor," she announced.

"Let him in."

Dahlia opened the door. Joe and Anita walked in.

Raymond welcomed his brother with a hug and said some words of greetings to Anita.

Anita could barely look at him straight in the eye. That was one of the reasons he detested being known as a billionaire. Suddenly, people would begin to see the need to impress him and get into his good grace. Anita would usually tease him and scold him if necessary, but now she couldn't even manage to look him in the face.

"What can I offer you to drink?" Dahlia asked.

Joe smiled. "Never mind. Maybe later. For now we've got a mess to clean up."

Dahlia gave an understanding smile and then sat next to Raymond.

Joe took his attention back to Raymond. "The board of directors called a meeting. From the look of things you're going to be the topic of discussion."

"They are not going to just impeach me because of this little scandal," Raymond argued. "I've worked hard. We've had 20% increase in profit since I joined Connor Corp. That should count for something."

Joe looked thoughtful, appearing almost sad. "I'm sorry, bro, but the board can impeach you."

Raymond pulled his brow together in a frown.

"Most of the directors were not happy when dad imposed you as the chairman of the board of directors. This is a huge opportunity for them to impeach you. They will attack your personality and say that you're not representing the brand well. The shareholders will start a petition against you. That wouldn't be difficult because

60% of our shareholders are women. And you know women can be sentimental about...you know what. If you don't want us to throw away what dad has worked for all these years, then we need a plan very quickly."

Raymond sighed and sank back into the couch. He truly was devastated. Although he was doing a very good job of not going into a raging outburst, inside he was barely holding up.

But getting back with Tamara, he didn't regret it. Never. Not for once. If he could, he would choose to be with Tamara again and again. Damn the consequence!

But he had to fix this. Tamara had built up her reputation for years and if this story ruined her career, he wouldn't forgive himself for it.

"What if I deny our affair... I mean how does it affect Tamara Price & Associates?" Raymond asked.

Anita cleared her throat. "If I may..."

Raymond gestured her to speak on. "Please, go ahead."

"Thank you. Right now, Tamara Price & Associates is facing hell. They've lost quite a lot of clients since the news broke. If you deny it, and people believe you, then it's a saving grace for Tamara Price & Associates."

"It would be good for Connor Corp if you deny it," Joe said. "Thankfully, in all the pictures they got, both of you weren't in any compromising position."

"Okay. Anita, please, go ahead and put the words out," Raymond said. "My relationship with

Tamara was purely professional. My wife and I had issues with our marriage. We hired Tamara to help fix it. She has been extremely helpful. And that's it."

"Okay," Anita replied. "Let's just hope people will believe the story."

"We can say that Tamara was extremely helpful and she was able to save our marriage," Dahlia added. "And then we can throw a party in celebration of our one year wedding anniversary. That will make it more believable."

"No way!" Raymond yelled.

"Actually, bro, it's a good idea," Joe said. "You should take it."

"Yes, it's a good idea. The story will be more believable," Anita added.

Raymond sighed. "Okay."

Joe let out a deep breath and turned to Dahlia. "Now, we can have that drink."

Their laughter roared through the room.

Raymond's voice stopped their laughs. "Joe, I know you really wanted to keep dad's legacy intact. You didn't want people to know that I'm a Connor. And I'm very sorry. I breach the agreement. Of course, if you want to take over everything, I'll..."

"Come on, brother. Forget about the agreement. That was a silly agreement in the first place. I'm grown now and for what it's worth, I'm proud to have you as a brother."

****

"Tamara, you got to hear this," Drake said, excitements written in his face and voice.

Tamara managed to give a smile. "Good news?"

"The word is out. Raymond claimed the relationship between both of you is strictly professional. You helped save their marriage, and sometime next week, they will be celebrating their one year wedding anniversary."

Tamara stared on into nothingness. History was repeating itself. After all the promises, Raymond was letting her down again. Tears gathered in her eyes.

"Tamara. It's good news. Megan is busy on the phone. Our clients are calling back. The people are taking back everything they said. It's good news."

She smiled sadly. "I'm happy. It's good news."

"It calls for celebration."

"Drinks are on me," Tamara said.

"Good! Let me go help Megan with the clients. After that, we will celebrate."

She nodded. "Okay."

Tears rolled down her cheeks immediately Drake got out of her office. Her heart ached so much she thought she might have an heart attack. Why should love hurts this much? Raymond denied her, hurt her. Again.

Such a fool she'd been. To have believed him. To have believed all his promises. He'd promised her forever. He'd promised her that whatever happened, his feelings for her wouldn't change.

The time they had shared, the love they'd made; it had been a lie. He had made a fool out of her. He'd used her like a piece of...trash to be thrown away.

Her tears stopped flowing. She stopped crying, but her heart was bleeding, aching terribly.

Few minutes later, her cell phone rang. It was Raymond.

She pressed the green button. "Are you calling to say you're sorry for denying me?"

"Mara..."

She cut him off. "You said whatever happens that you'd be on my side."

"I'm on your side, Mara."

"You said whatever happens your feelings for me won't change."

"It didn't change. I love you. I'm in love with you."

"You know what? I'm done listening to your lies. Get the hell off my phone. We are over! Don't let me see you again!"

She dropped the call angrily.

Chapter 25

In the garage, Raymond cranked the key in the ignition and pulled onto the street, tires squealing in sympathetic anger. He drove speedily down to Tamara's office. As he drove, there was only one thing on his mind. He didn't want to lose Tamara. Not again.

He pulled up at the parking lot and hurried into the building. He walked into the lobby and met Tamara, Drake and Megan, holding a cup of wine. They were probably celebrating the end of the small storm that almost ruined the law firm.

"Hello," he said, greeting everyone.

Without waiting for any response, he took the glass of wine away from Tamara and placed it on the table.

"Ray, what are you doing?" Her voice wasn't harsh. And she was breathing heavily.

Raymond didn't respond. He held her by the wrist and dragged her along. Tamara didn't resist. He was much stronger than her. So, resistance would be futile and wouldn't do her no good.

When they had walked into Tamara's office, Raymond let go of her. "What were you talking about on the phone?"

She folded her arms and looked away, letting him know she had an attitude. "I don't know."

He closed his eyes and grimaced like he was in pain. Then he opened them again. "What I did, denying our relationship, I did it for you. I couldn't sit back and watch your career gets destroyed."

"Screw career! You know I would give it up over and over again just to be with you. So don't give me that line that you did it for me, because I don't buy it."

"I did it for you!"

Annoyance cut through her. "I don't believe you," she yelled. "You did it for you. You chose your position at Connor Corp. You chose Dahlia. Again!" she emphasized 'again'.

"Dammit, Mara," he roared.

He scared her. She pulled away avoiding his gaze.

"I'm sorry," he said, his voice gentler. "I shouldn't have shouted at you."

She folded her arms tight across her chest. She was hurting badly and she felt the need to let it all out. So she did.

"I gave you a second chance and you screwed it up. I believed your lies. I let you use me. I let you make a fool out of me for the second time."

"Oh! So this is still about Dahlia, huh?" he asked bitterly.

"Yes. Yes. It's about her. You chose her."

"I never chose Dahlia. Not one year ago. Not now! I want to tell you what happened..."

"No. No. I don't want to know," she said and began to walk away.

He caught up with her and threw himself in front of her, holding her upper arms and staring down into her eyes. "You remember my trip to Dallas, the one you couldn't go with me because you had to be at the court for your client."

She scowled. "So you're trying to say you went to Dahlia because I wasn't there for you."

He shook his head. "No, Mara. I'm saying I was with Dahlia because I'm a fool. An idiot."

She was a bit calmer.

So he continued, "When I first took over as CEO of Connor Corp, we were running at loss instead of making profit. The shareholders were complaining. I went on a business trip to Dallas and I made the wrong call. Everything my father worked for was going down the drain and I didn't know how to save it. I went to a bar for a drink or two, you know, just to clear my head. I had only taken two glasses when I saw Dahlia walked into the bar. I knew she was your friend. I greeted her and she sat with me. I bought her a drink and we started to talk. Before I knew it, I had too much alcohol. Dahlia offered to drive me back to my hotel and...and..." he stuttered, slowly releasing his hold on her upper arms.

Tamara could see the pain, deep down inside his eyes.

He paused for a moment and swallowed hard. "I fixed the problems at Connor Corp. I quit drinking too much. But the most important thing that got destroyed that night, I've not been able to fix it."

Tamara didn't say anything for a while, her only answer a sigh.

The room was dead silent. Tears filled Tamara eyes just like it filled his. Her heart ached just like his.

She held back the tears. "I understand that it was just one weak moment. It was one mistake. But you didn't have to marry her."

"When I came back from Dallas, I couldn't tell you what I did. I couldn't own up to my mistake." He paused for a moment, but he avoided looking at her. "Few months after, I went on a business trip to Paris. I saw Dahlia. Again. She told me the thing we did had become a baby. She was pregnant."

Tamara sank her head in her palm. "No!"

"You know how much it hurt me that my father rejected me. Even now, after my father accepted me, I'm still the illegitimate child of James Connor. I didn't want to give that fate to my son. I didn't choose Dahlia, I chose my son. I married Dahlia in Paris. I thought if I tried, I might love Dahlia. I thought it was possible to give my son a home where his mother and his father would live happily together. I wanted to dedicate myself to my marriage. I wanted to do the right thing, be an honorable man. I tried. But Dahlia kept ruining all my effort. I began to connect the dots. Dahlia didn't just happen to find me at the bar in Dallas. She followed me there. We didn't just run into each other at Paris, she followed me. My relationship with Dahlia was pre-planned by whoever she receives her order from. And I fell for the trap."

Tamara didn't respond, so he continued, "After my failed effort, I was able to understand and forgive my father for rejecting me. It is true that a parent should do everything and anything for his child, but, sometimes, it is necessary to look for one's happiness first. Someday, I know my son would understand."

The room was dead silent again and almost suffocating. Raymond could feel the tension pulling them apart.

It was soothing to know that Ray hadn't willingly betrayed her, but still...

She leaned closer to him, looking him straight in the eye. "Ray..."she said quietly, her voice slightly above a whisper. "I love you. I'll fight your battles, I'll dry your tears, I'll die for you, I'll do anything for you, but I'm not sure if you will do the same for me. And..." she paused for a second, trying to figure out the best way to say what's on her mind. But then she knew no matter how nice she phrased it, her words wouldn't sound nice to Raymond's ears. So, she just let it out.

"I want to be with you, I really want to. But I want to be more than a mistress to you. I want to be your one and only choice. Not a second choice after a failed marriage. I deserve more than to be a mistress to any man. So, if you love me as much as you claim, if you want to be with me, you need to choose me. But until you do, we're over!"

She finished her speech and looked at him. He looked wounded and brokenhearted.

Walking over to the door, she held open the door, trying desperately not to cry. Not yet.

Just hold out a little while longer, she told herself.

Then he walked over to her, held her face in his palm and placed a heartbreakingly gentle kiss on her lips.

She didn't respond to his kiss. Not that she didn't want to— she wanted to melt into him and say *you know what, screw everything I said, I am yours.*

But she couldn't. Not after that big speech about how she deserved more than to be a mistress.

He pulled away from her and looked into her eyes for a split second.

And then he was gone.

She heard him saying goodbye to Drake and Megan, and she heard the front door open and shut.

And then she let the hot tears rolled down.

Chapter 26

The following morning, Tamara didn't want to get up from bed. As usual, her response to heartbreaks was to just sleep it away.

No matter how hard she tried, she couldn't get Raymond off her mind. She remembered how they had made love on this damn bed. Her throat tightened as she fought back the tears that wouldn't stop flowing since she ended things with Raymond.

And then she remembered the love letter he wrote her the morning after that night. Rolling over to her back, she stretched out a hand to open the drawer. She grabbed the letter and read again:

Baby,

You slept like a baby, didn't want to wake you up. I had to leave early cos I had some business to attend to. I'll see you at lunch.

Oh! Place an ice on your ankle if it still hurts, or else...you won't be able to put on those Chrysler

Building heels today.

Kisses,
Ray.

When she finished reading, her heart broke again into a thousand tiny little pieces. And she burst into relentless tears.

Ending things with Raymond was the right thing to do. She knew she did the right thing, but why did it have to hurt this much?

She consoled herself that Raymond would come back for her. His silence didn't mean he was done with her. He would come back for her, she knew that.

She stayed in bed from morning till evening. She skipped breakfast and skipped lunch. When evening came, she decided to get up from bed and eat something.

As she got out of bed, her thoughts went to Drake. On a day like this, he was always around to force her out of bed and helped her get through the heartbreak. She wondered why he didn't show up to force her out of bed. Perhaps, he was too busy at work.

She opened the door of her bedroom only to find a rose flower on the table at the center of her living room.

Raymond?

Quickly, she ran to the table and picked it up. She held the rose to her nose and her lips curved into a small smile. And then she noticed a small card attached to the flower. She opened and read very quickly.

I want to put a smile on your pretty face.

She smiled. You did put a smile on my face, she said in her heart.

"Have dinner with me, Tamara."

She trembled and turned back to see who it was.

"D...Drake," she stuttered. "How did you get in?"

Okay. She knew that was a stupid question. Drake had always been able to come into her house.

Drake didn't respond.

She looked at him.

He wore a black suit on white shirt and red tie. His hair was neatly cut and his face was as handsome as she had always known it to be.

"Did you...? You know, did you send this?"

Hands in his pockets, he nodded with a kind of attractive arrogance. And then he walked closer to her.

"I love you, Tamara. Please, have dinner with me."

Tamara's heart beat faster than ever. She sucked in her breath as Drake's words came back to her.

When I ask you out for dinner or buy you a rose, then you should worry.

He had bought her a rose, and was now asking her out for dinner. Definitely, it was time to worry. Drake...loved her.

"Since when, Drake. Since when have you loved me?"

"Since the very first moment I set my eyes on you."

She stared wide-eyed. Her voice caught up in her throat for a second. And when she finally found her voice, she was breathing so hard. "Since high school? And...y...you never said anything."

"I never had the chance. In high school, you had a boyfriend and I didn't want to ruin your relationship. And when you left him, you met Raymond. I've never really had a chance."

"But I've always seen you like a brother."

He raised his shoulders in a shrug. "You can always unseen me like a brother."

"Drake! I can't."

"Why? You ended things with Raymond. Didn't you?"

"Yes, I did. But my heart didn't do what I want it to do. My heart is still with Raymond. As long as my heart..."

He cut him off. "I get it. As long as your heart is still with Raymond, you can't be with me."

She nodded.

He took the rejection calmly, his face clear of all emotions. "Come here," he said. He wasn't asking. It was more like an order.

Tamara walked closer to where he stood.

Taking his hands out of his pocket, he held her in his arms.

She felt safe in his arms and never before has she felt so dependent.

Gently, he brushed her hair to the back with his fingers and placed a soft kiss on her forehead. "I understand. Okay? It's just that Raymond keep hurting you and it pained me that me, the best guy in the world, is in love with you and you can't see it."

Tamara stifled a grin. "The best guy in the world?"

He winked at her. "I am the best."

She smiled. "Your ego is bigger than Mars itself."

He smiled sadly. "You still owe me a dinner, you know."

She nodded, smiling. "I owe you."

"I guess it's not going to be this night."

She nodded again.

"Okay." He held her in his arms again. "Goodnight, Tamara," he whispered.

"Goodnight."

He pulled away and began to walk to the door.

"Are you going to be okay?" Tamara asked.

He smirked. "You're kidding, right? Drake Johnson is always okay."

She smiled. "I forgot."

He smiled and then he was gone.

Drake didn't like showing vulnerability, but Tamara knew he was hurt and he was doing a good job of hiding it. Rejection, that was what he was feeling, and she ached for him.

The man had always been there for her and she felt bad for rejecting him. But it was better that way. Better than raising his hopes by going out with him.

She walked to the kitchen, poured herself a glass of wine and then walked back to the bedroom. Immediately she walked into the bedroom, her cell phone rang.

She pressed the green button. "Hello…"

"Hello, Miss Price, it's Dr. Morgan. I'm calling to let you know the results of the toxin test are out."

"Really?"

"Yes. You said to call you immediately we have the result."

"Yes. Yes. Please, tell me. What does the result say?"

"Well, the hair strand tested positive for Arsenic."

"What?"

"It's still quite very low in your body, however, if you keep exposing yourself to it, you'll be dead in less than three months. Meanwhile, you should come in to the hospital for hemodialysis. It's going to remove the arsenic from your bloodstream. After that, we might have to get you on Chelation therapy."

"Okay, doc. Thanks," she said and hung up.

Dr. Morgan must have thought the hair sample belonged to her. But that didn't matter.

Raymond was a walking corpse.

She was trembling as if she'd just received a death sentence for Raymond. She knew that the doctor said the arsenic poisoning wasn't chronic and could still be treated with hemodialysis, yet it felt as if Raymond was dead already.

She had secretly hoped that Raymond would

be right, that Dahlia was incapable of hurting Raymond and that the test would come out negative. But her hopes had been dashed with just one phone call.

She burst into tears and was wailing like a wounded animal. After all the tears she had shed, she didn't think she had any left. Obviously, she was wrong.

Trying to hold back her tears, she told herself that crying was unnecessary and wouldn't solve the problem.

Quickly, she took her cell phone and placed a call to Raymond.

"Ray, where are you? I need to see you immediately. It's very important. I need to tell you something. Please be here..."

"Calm down, Mara. I'm around the corner. I was on my way to your place when your call came in."

She let out a breath. "Okay."

"I'll be there in a few."

She hung up.

She sat frozen, holding her breath as she waited for Raymond. She was desperately thinking about how best to break the news to Raymond. What could be the best way to tell a man that his wife, the mother of his son had been contaminating his food with arsenic poison?

She heard the doorbell rang and she ran to the door.

As she yanked open the door, as she set her eyes on Raymond, relief coursed through her. Seeing him reminded her that Raymond was still alive. He wasn't dead yet. And she wouldn't be able to live if he died.

With a sob, she flew into his arms and kissed him, moaning with pleasure as his arms enfolded her.

After a while, Raymond broke the kiss and pulled away. Holding her upper arms, he studied her, looking her straight in the eyes. "Mara, are you okay?" he asked, seeing the worry in her eyes.

She shook her head. "I don't want to lose you. Not now. Not ever."

His surprise was so obvious. But he bent down and gave her a melting kiss that pulled the pieces of her heart back together.

Shivers of desire and need overcame her and she pulled him toward the couch, bringing him down on top of her. "I love you," she whispered.

His eyes grew hungry. "I love you too, Mara. I love you too too much," he whispered as he pulled his woman lovingly into his arms.

SPECIAL SNEEK PREVIEW

On the following pages you will find a brief excerpt from

I

Choose

You

the sequel to When Love Hurts.

****

Tamara Price had always considered herself to be a very smart, canny and intelligent woman. Yet with all her intelligence, she wasn't able to protect Raymond from being poisoned. She wasn't even able to convince Raymond that his wife, Dahlia, was responsible for contaminating his food with tiny bit of Arsenic and she intended to keep doing it until the substance kills him.

Now she had no choice than to play her last card.

It was an unpleasant task but Tamara needed to do it tonight.

Sitting in her car parked at the parking lot of Mosaic nightclub, Tamara gazed out through the night-darkened window, her eyes scanning for any sign of Dahlia.

The thought of what she was about to do sickened her and she felt an irritation in her stomach. Trying to control the itch to throw up, she held her breath. Then she consoled herself that she was doing it for Raymond.

A car parked opposite of her and from the license plate, she could tell it was Dahlia.

Gently, Tamara took her cell phone, got out of the car and walked toward Dahlia's car. Cautiously, she opened the passenger door and got in, placing her cell phone on the center console of the car as she sat.

"You wanted to talk," Dahlia said, her steely, cold eyes gazing at her.

"Yes," Tamara replied.

"What is it? I've got only little time to spare."

Tamara's blood boiled in rage. Her fist clenched and her eyes flashed with fire. She wanted to say, *you know what, screw you!* But then she calmed down, reminding herself that she was doing this for Raymond.

"You win. I lose," Tamara said quietly. The words took a long moment to come out of her mouth, but when it did she wished she could take it all back. She never had to accept defeat ever before, especially not to her arch-enemy. But there was always a first time for everything.

Putting her hand to her ear, Dahlia leaned closer. "What did you say?"

Tamara sucked in her breath. "You win. I lose," she repeated.

Dahlia gave a loud laugh without humor, beating the steering wheel as she did. "And it took you this long to know that I always win. How did you realize it?"

"You threatened to destroy the two things I loved most—Raymond and my job. My career almost got destroyed when you broke that news and now Raymond tested positive for Arsenic poison. You did it, I'm sure."

"Of course, I did it." She looked over and gave another of her dry laugh. "*If you so much as hurt Raymond or even pull a strand of hair from his body, I will track you down. I will hunt you and I will rain down a godly lake that burns with fire and brimstone upon you,*" she said, mimicking the way Tamara said it. "You remember when you threatened me like that."

Tamara shut her eyes and forced out a tear. "I'm sorry, Dahlia. I am truly sorry."

"I feel on top of the world right now," Dahlia said. "The strong, powerful Tamara Price, accepting defeat. I'm definitely on top of the world."

"Dahlia, please. Spare Raymond's life. I promise I'll handle your divorce well. I'll make sure you get half, if not all, of the Connor wealth. But Raymond doesn't have to die. Please…"

"Tamara, I wish it is that simple," Dahlia, said, her countenance suddenly soft as if Tamara had started a sensitive conversation. She looked at Tamara and blinked. "You see, our one year wedding anniversary party is in ten days from today. Raymond will be dead on or before that day."

Tamara didn't have to force the tears out. It came freely. Placing her hand over Dahlia's, she looked into her eyes and pleaded. "Dahlia, please. Spare Raymond's life. Not for my sake, but for your son's sake. You said you don't want him to grow up without a father, right? For your son's sake, please, spare his life. If it pleases you, I'll stay away from him. Raymond will be for you and your son alone. Even if we are not together, I'm happy as long as he is alive somewhere."

Dahlia looked thoughtful, almost sad. "You love him very much, don't you?"

Tamara nodded gently.

Dahlia smiled sadly. "I love him too," she said. And then the smile disappeared. "But this is beyond me. It's more than me." Her voice became very shaky. "Everything has been planned. It's not in my hands to decide if Raymond should live or die. I don't want him dead too." Tears filled her eyes and she blinked it back. "Let's just keep praying so that maybe by miracle, he might live."

"Dahlia, please," Tamara pleaded.

Too close to tears to speak further, Dahlia swallowed the lumps in her throat. "Goodnight, Tamara. And please, pray well."

Tamara took her phone and left Dahlia's car. When she got back to her car, she found the voice recorder on her phone and hit the play button.

You threatened to destroy the two things I loved most—Raymond and my job. My career almost got destroyed when you broke that news and now Raymond tested positive for Arsenic poison. You did it, I'm sure."

"Of course, I did it."

She pressed the stop button and smiled to herself. Task completed. Dahlia had a lot to answer for.

Message to my readers

Hello there! Thank you for reading WHEN LOVE HURTS.

If you enjoyed it, would you mind leaving a review on Amazon? It can be only two to three sentences, nothing fancy. Good reviews really do help authors out, so if you don't mind, I would be very grateful!

If you would like to be notified when there are new releases by me, please subscribe to my website (www.authoraderonke.com).

And if you just want to say hi to me, email me at authoraderonke@yahoo.com. I love hearing from my readers. Believe me, when you've wondered if anybody out there actually enjoys reading your book, it's a relief to hear from people who enjoyed it. It encourages me to keep writing.

I'll have I Choose You (When Love Hurts, #2) ready early January next year. (Edit: I Choose You is now available!)

Thank you again for reading my books.

Aderonke Moyinlorun
Facebook: @AderonkeMoyinlorun
Twitter: @IAmAderonke
Website: www.authoraderonke.com